Manless in Montclair

Manless in Montclair

A NOVEL

How a Happily
Married Woman
Became a Widow
Looking for Love
in the Wilds of Suburbia

AMY HOLMAN EDELMAN

Shaye Areheart Books • New York

Published in the United States by Shaye Areheart Books, an imprint of the
Crown Publishing Group, a division of Random House, Inc., New York.

www.crownpublishing.com

Shaye Areheart Books with colophon is a registered trademark
of Random House, Inc.

Grateful acknowledgment is made to Alfred Publishing Co., Inc.,
for permission to reprint an excerpt from "Christmas in Prison" by John Prine,
copyright © 1973 (Renewed) by Walden Music, Inc., and Sour Grapes Music.
All rights administered by WB Music Corp. All rights reserved.
Reprinted by permission of Alfred Publishing Co., Inc.

Library of Congress Cataloging-in-Publication Data

Edelman, Amy Holman.

Manless in Montclair : how a happily married woman
became a widow looking for love in the wilds of suburbia /
by Amy Edelman

1. Chick lit.   I. Title.

PS3605.D43M36 2007

813'.6—dc22   2007017951

ISBN 978-0-307-23695-1

Printed in the United States of America

Design by Maria Elias

10 9 8 7 6 5 4 3 2

First Edition

This book is dedicated to

the memory of

my grandmother Miriam, who taught me about beauty;

my father, Richard, who taught me the importance of appreciating every day;

my husband, David, who taught me about love;

Sophie and Catie, who make every day worthwhile;

and

Phil, who showed me there is such a thing as a real-life happy ending.

ACKNOWLEDGMENTS

To my longtime agent, friend, and goddess, Lisa Bankoff, for her tenacity and belief in my talents, and to her invaluable goddess-in-training, Tina Wexler. To my publisher, Shaye Areheart, and my editor, Deborah Artman (the heroine of this book would have been five inches taller but for her), for trusting that I could actually do this.

This book would not have been possible without the love and support of my incredible and extended family: the Holmans, the Masons, the Kaplans, the Edelmans, the Bukzins, the Quinns, and the Leos.

To my friends, old and new (you know who you are), whose love and support have made the best times better and the worst times bearable. I am truly blessed to have you all in my life.

For Jean Chemay, Michael Bukzin, Donna Benner, Irv Rosen, Phil Leo, Rion Dugan, Delsenia Glover, and Mom, early readers whose feedback was reassuring and invaluable.

To Steven, for getting me through. For Cindy Erdesohn, for getting me *and* the kids through. For Ann Bird, for helping me sort it all out. For Irv Rosen, for his real-life support and for inspiring the great guy Isabel ends up with.

To Corky Siemaszko and Maki Becker, for making me famous.

And to the exceptional publicists at Weber Shandwick, whose regular freelance work (and ensuing paychecks) enabled me to have the time I needed to write this book.

Manless in Montclair

CHAPTER ONE

It was another hot and humid afternoon in August. A fine sheen covered everything, lending ordinary people a glow usually associated with saints and supermodels. Even my parquet floors were sweating.

At 2:15 I left my husband and went to the dentist to have my teeth whitened. Michael was sleeping when I left. He had been suffering for days from a chronic headache, and I thought it best not to wake him. I expected to be home in about an hour.

I swept back into our apartment at 3:45, teeth gleaming. The first thing I noticed was a wicked smell, like rubber burning on a hot sidewalk. Michael had gone to the acupuncturist the day before, seeking relief from his headache and, from past experience with such remedies, I assumed he must have brewed her special tea. I bypassed the living room and walked down the hall to our bedroom, where I'd left Michael sleeping an hour and a half before.

Our blue and white paisley duvet lay crumpled on the bed, but Michael was no longer under it. The air conditioner beckoned me with a loud rumble, and I stood in front of it for a moment, letting the stale breeze cool my skin. Sufficiently chilled, I turned and walked back down the hall into the heavier air of our living room. It was then that I saw him, lying at the foot of the green overstuffed chair, a few inches away from his favorite perch on the wellworn, beige linen sofa. Except for the small pool of blood that had formed on the rug beside his head, he looked as if he might still be sleeping.

I ran past Michael to the far end of the room, my heart beating hard in my throat. I rummaged through the papers and notebooks that covered my desk in search of the portable phone. Finding it, I dialed 911. After what felt like enough time to grow old in, a dispassionate voice finally came on to the line.

"I think my husband is dead," I said, shaking. There was no thought. Just words and sweat and panic. "What should I do?"

"Why do you think he's dead?" asked the woman, sounding slightly bored. I looked at Michael, shirtless on the floor. His skin, always fair and freckled, had turned an unnatural shade of lavender. And he was quiet. I had slept beside Michael for a dozen years, and he always snored like a water buffalo. Now, except for the crazy pounding in my chest, the silence was deafening. And finally, Michael was normally such a light sleeper. If he weren't dead, surely in all this commotion he would have woken up by now.

"I'm pretty sure he's dead," I replied, digging my nails into my palms in an effort to keep from screaming. "Tell me what to do."

The woman gave me instructions as if speaking to a ten-year-old. And like any good child, I did as I was told. I performed mouth-to-mouth and thought fleetingly that Michael's lips still felt warm against mine. I lifted his callused hand and touched his wrist, feeling for a pulse.

He was still.

I felt numb.

"There's no change," I told the 911 operator. And then, clearly running out of options, I called on God for a miracle—a sudden gasp for breath, a fluttering of the eyelids. The woman instructed me to push on Michael's chest, and I inadvertently hung up the phone to do so.

Push.

Nothing.

How did this happen? Just a few days ago I was telling my best friend Phoebe how unexpectedly well my life was going. She was right, I thought dejectedly. I should have spit. Because in the time it took to get my teeth a whiter shade of white, it was all gone, my guts in a knot as I knelt beside my motionless husband.

Push.

Nothing.

I needed further instructions. As long as I was doing something, I thought, there was still room for hope. I reached for the phone just as it began to ring. Could it be the 911 operator calling *me*?

"Hello?" I answered hopefully.

"Hi, Isabel!" said my upstairs neighbor Ivana in her heavy Serbian accent. "What are you doing?"

On most days my response would have been "Nothing,

much . . . what about you?" But today was not most days. "Actually," I said, "I'm sitting on the floor next to Michael. I think
he's dead."

And I was, to put it simply, a mess.

"You open your eyes. It's dark. Your knees, which are pressed
against your chest, begin to throb. The air is thick and your back
hurts. But it isn't until you try to raise an arm to scratch your nose
that you realize you're folded up in a tiny little box like a cheap
piece of goods from Wal-Mart."

It was three o'clock on a warm August afternoon, and my
best friend Phoebe and I were sitting in a bar drinking frozen mar-
garitas. Phoebe was reading a quiz from a recent issue of *Cosmopoli-
tan* magazine, which proposed to determine our Sexuality Index.

"Then what happens?" I asked, leaning over, trying to get a
glimpse of the page.

"Then you wake up. If you're me," she added, "there's probably a little drool on the pillow."

"That's disgusting." I reached for a corn chip. "What do you
think it means?"

"The drool?"

"No, Phoebe. The dream."

From a strictly aesthetic point of view, Phoebe drew eyes like
a tall, blonde magnet, so strikingly beautiful it was impossible to
look away. She shrugged her slender shoulders.

"Damned if I know," she replied. "But, lucky us. We get to

choose from the following: (a) You've just had a great night of sex. (b) You *need* to have a great night of sex. (c) You're *afraid* to have a great night of sex."

Phoebe looked at me expectantly.

"Jeez," I replied. "What's sex?"

"Been that long, huh?" she asked, pen waving. "I'm going for 'my apartment's too small.' "

"Is that one of the choices?"

"No," Phoebe answered. "But it should be. How about you?"

"I dunno. It sounds to me a lot like my childhood."

"The drool?" Phoebe asked.

I shook my head. "The metaphor. Tiny box. Small spaces. Confining to the point of suffocation."

She ran her finger down the page of the magazine. "Those don't seem to be listed either."

"OK. Try this. *Invasion of the Body Snatchers* with an all-Jewish, all-white-bread-eating, all-middle-class cast."

"And people say I'm dramatic," said Phoebe, tossing her head dramatically. "Sounds boring to me."

"Hmmm," I replied. "More like claustrophobic."

In actuality, I had spent most of my childhood living *outside* the Wal-Mart box. My friend's parents were married. Mine were divorced after a period of dissatisfaction best described as operatic. My mom, younger sister, and I lived in a garden apartment—a step below the relative luxury of everyone else's identical three-bedroom row house. And, in what constituted the deepest cut of all, in contrast to my taller, slimmer, straighter-haired classmates, my hair frizzed at the slightest hint of humidity and my body was too curvy to jam into the era's de rigueur tube tops and hip-hugger jeans.

I had vague aspirations of finding validation in the guise of success, a goal that usually lent itself to an individual possessing a certain amount of stature. But netting out at a meager five-feet nothing, I had little of the inborn force and magnetism native to those of more impressive heights.

By the time I reached college, I realized that even if I *had* possessed the brains of a giant and the wisdom of the ages, they'd have had to be squeezed down and vacuum-packed to fit the dimensions of my tiny storage space. It was hard enough in a man's world to be a woman of authority. As a petite woman with big boobs and a total inability to walk in heels, I feared I might never have a chance.

Three years after moving to New York City with my bachelor of arts degree, I was still unable to find my niche. Stints in retail and clothing design revealed a lack of talent and a shortage of patience (I had the drive, but I just couldn't figure out the direction). They also paid barely enough to cover my meager expenses. At an age when most of my peers were sprinting down the fast track, I was metaphorically curled up in a fetal position, still unsure of what I wanted to be when I grew up. I had found, to my dismay, that life was still about adjusting—trying to make jobs, jeans, and boyfriends fit.

At least, I told myself—sucking thoughtfully on a lime—I had some company. Phoebe had dreams of becoming an actress, but she didn't hesitate to concede that she'd be happy to settle for a rich, handsome doctor, should one become available to her. In order to pay the bills, we had indentured ourselves to a trendy dining establishment on the Upper East Side, where we earned our keep serving chopped salad and cheesecake to scotch-drinking, blue-haired socialites.

"Well," Phoebe said, adding up her final score with resignation. "It looks like my Sexuality Index is lower than my income."

"I very much doubt it."

As if on cue, the bartender came over to ogle Phoebe and check our progress with the drinks. She feigned interest; his eyes left her face only long enough to salt the glasses.

"Why don't you go after him?" Phoebe suggested, waving her lip-gloss wand in Kevin's direction as he retreated to the tequila.

"As if," I told her, reaching for another chip. It was not lost on me that if my vice were tobacco rather than salty snacks, I might have less trouble getting Kevin's attention. But I had grown used to being overlooked—by bartenders, sales clerks, and taxi drivers— especially while in the company of taller, prettier companions. "Besides," I added philosophically to my friend, "I have bigger things planned."

Phoebe arched her perfectly shaped brows. "I dunno . . . from what I hear there ain't too many bigger than Kevin's."

We left the bar a couple of hours later, pleasantly buzzed and blinking in the late afternoon sun. Hungry, we decided to pick up dinner at Michael's, a kosher-style, take-out chicken joint down the street from my apartment. The place, no larger than a walk-in closet, was buzzing with activity and redolent with the smells of grandma's cooking. Display cases on the right side were jammed with trays of raisin-studded noodle pudding, stuffed cabbage in tomato sauce, chopped liver, and cherry-red Jell-O. The left side of the store was at least ten degrees warmer and featured three large rotisserie machines filled with roasted chicken and crispy duck, their juices dripping rhythmically into the pans below. Customers at the front of the line shouted out their orders while, pressed close behind, a sea of tired and hungry people, mouths watering, stood waiting to be served.

"Maybe we should just get a pizza," I said loudly, eyeing the masses.

"Check . . . behind . . . counter," Phoebe mouthed, looking over in said direction.

"What?" I hollered back above the din.

"The guy behind the counter. *Check out the guy behind the counter.*"

"Cute, but isn't he about seventy?" I followed her gaze to the elderly gentleman quartering what looked to be a capon.

"Not *that* guy! The one with the pierced ear standing next to him."

He was about 5'8", strong arms, beautiful hands, eyes the color of a cloudless blue sky. I had noticed him during my regular chicken run the week before. As he answered to the name Michael, I assumed he was the owner of the establishment.

"Well, he *is* handling a knife," I told her, watching as he cut up a chicken, "but I doubt he makes as much money as an orthopedic surgeon."

We waited our turn, the crowd parted, and we stood—Phoebe a head and a half taller than me—at the front of the line.

"What'll it be, ladies?" Michael asked. His eyes took in Phoebe and then fell onto mine. And, surprisingly, they stayed there. And then he smiled. A sweet smile.

His sudden attention made my skin burn.

"A rich husband," answered Phoebe, smiling mischievously.

"Come again?" he asked, confused.

"Half a chicken, please," I said, shooting Phoebe what I hoped was a threatening look. It slid off her impossibly high cheekbones and landed on the dirty linoleum floor like a pile of creamed spinach.

When Michael turned his back to retrieve our chicken from the grease-splattered machine, Phoebe—perhaps due to her elevated alcohol levels—couldn't hold back. "He likes you!" she blurted. "Ask him out!"

"I told you . . ." I said, turning to face her. Phoebe was about 5'8" in heels, and my eyes landed somewhere in the vicinity of her collarbone.

"I *know*," she said with exasperation. "You have *bigger* things planned. But he *is* cute, you're not dating anyone, you can't cook, and I think you'd look adorable together." And before I could stop her, she asked him if he would deliver.

"I can do that," said Michael, nodding in my direction. "But I need your phone number in order to arrange it."

He took a pen from behind his ear and offered it to me, along with a menu and the plastic bag that contained my order. Cornered, I took the bag and the pen and scribbled my number on the menu, even though we all knew that I was already holding half a chicken and a quarter pound of cucumber salad in my sweaty little hands.

CHAPTER TWO

The EMS guys took their time walking down the hall toward my door. They entered my living room as if they had merely stopped by for a cup of coffee. They set down their equipment leisurely and finally tried to revive my husband. I had seen five seasons of *ER*. And *The Sopranos*. Despite my actions to the contrary, I was pretty sure Michael was dead the moment I saw him.

The police got there shortly after the EMS. Once they arrived I was expected to do something more than sit on the floor protectively beside my husband. I felt vaguely like Maria in *West Side Story* when the Jets arrive to take Tony's body away. "Don't you *touch* him," I felt like screaming.

There were questions of timing and whereabouts. What was my dentist's phone number, and what time had the appointment been? Why wasn't Michael at work? How long had he been having headaches?

The cops inspected the smelly pot of tea, as if death may have been caused by tainted Lipton. They asked for names, phone numbers, birth dates. When they were finished asking questions, they gently suggested that I contact our family. When I failed to stand up—I had a suspicion my legs might fail to support me—they politely insisted.

My first call was to Phoebe.

"Phoebe, it's me."

"Who?"

"What do you mean 'who'? It's Izzy."

Pause.

"Michael's dead."

"What do you mean Michael's dead?"

"I mean he died, Phoebe. Michael died."

"You're kidding me."

"No. I'm not. Michael is dead."

"He is not dead."

"Yes, Phoebe. He is."

"Is this a joke?"

I walked into the kitchen, raising my voice in hopes of getting this simple idea across to her. "PHOEBE. MICHAEL IS DEAD. ON THE FLOOR. IN OUR LIVING ROOM." Then I kicked a cabinet for good measure.

"Oh my God. What happened? Was it a heart attack?"

"I don't know," I responded, exhausted from the effort. "And they're not telling."

"I'll be right over."

Next I tried my sister Wendy, who had taken the kids to the Jersey shore. I was relieved when she didn't answer, having no earthly idea what I was going to say.

I kept my neighbor Ivana at bay until after the police and EMS departed. A tall Buddhist with silver gray hair, she arrived offering comfort, homemade apple strudel, and herbal tea. But this was no time for snacks—there were people still to call, decisions to be made. When would the funeral be held? What, in heaven's name, should Michael wear? I was told it would be at least an hour until the medical examiner arrived. In the meantime, Michael lay peacefully on the pale pink rug in the middle of our living room. It was almost a comfort to see him there, his neck still warm to my touch.

I hadn't eaten all day and began to feel nauseous. The Caesar salad I had brought home with me sat on the kitchen counter like a relic from another age. I forced down a banana, which came back up half an hour later. It was the last thing I would eat for four days. Unsure of what to do next, I retreated to my bathroom, gaining little comfort from the piles of shoes and handbags that—being short on closet space—surrounded me there.

"You should wear heels," said Phoebe, running a critical eye up and down my ensemble.

"I tip over in heels."

"Jeez, Isabel . . . it's your first date with the guy, a cute, potentially rich chicken store owner. What are you gonna wear? Sneakers?"

Despite two years studying clothing design, my style sense was limited to critiquing what other people wore. So Phoebe helped me dig through my closet for something she deemed suitable: black cotton capris, a lacy T-shirt, and black mules.

"Two inches is better than nothing," Phoebe said over her shoulder, tossing the shoes in my direction, "which, incidentally, is the same thing an old boyfriend tried to tell me on the occasion of our first time. And let me tell you something, Izzy . . . was he ever *wrong.*"

"I'll keep that in mind," I answered.

"Explain something to me," Phoebe asked, now on the hunt for a handbag.

"Yeah?"

"This song," she said, pointing her chin in the direction of the turntable. " *'It's a happy enchilada and you think you're gonna drown?'* "

"Phoebe," I answered, frustrated with the effort of trying to button the capris, "it's a John Prine song. The words are *'it's a half an inch of water,'* not 'happy enchilada.' "

"Oh," she said, satisfied. "That makes more sense then."

I tried to smooth down the waves in my thick brown hair and, as per Phoebe, brushed on an extra coat of mascara.

"You look like a little Jewish femme fatale," she said, giving me the once-over.

"As opposed to what? A large Catholic one?"

Either way, I saw no such vision as I stared at my reflection. I squared my shoulders, nevertheless, and tried to channel a little of Katharine Hepburn's brittle self-confidence.

"The whole thing says sexy-but-not-trying-too-hard," Phoebe assured me.

"As long as it doesn't say desperately-trying-to-pick-up-men-in-chicken-stores," I said, applying a final swipe of "Better Than Nude" lip gloss.

Phoebe left at 6:45, and my intercom buzzed at precisely seven. I walked carefully to the door (trying to get used to the heels), pushed the button, and counted to five before opening it. It was a week since my last encounter with Michael, and I hoped he was as cute as I remembered him. He didn't disappoint, standing before me wearing jeans, a light blue T-shirt, and a shy smile. He wasn't, I further noted, even breathing hard. I had been living in my apartment for almost three years, and the ascent still left me panting.

"You're not even breathing hard," I marveled.

"Sure I am. I'm just doing it quietly so you can't hear me."

"You must be in really good shape. There are thirty-two steps, not counting the outside stoop. Most of the time I need to take a nap when I get to the top."

"Don't feel bad," he said as I stood aside to let him through the door. "I work part-time as a personal trainer."

It showed.

Michael and his muscular body stood in my living room while I went in search of a sweater.

"Nice place," he said, absently brushing some dust off the windowsill.

"Smaller than what I hoped for but I guess it'll do for now," I answered, sweater in hand. "How big is yours?"

The words were out of my mouth before I realized how they must have sounded.

"Big enough," he replied dryly.

I felt my face flush and realized I needn't have bothered with the rouge.

We grabbed a taxi and headed to Azora, a restaurant Michael suggested on the Upper West Side. I was used to *serving* fine food, not actually ingesting it, and the prospect of eating something besides dry leftovers and takeout chicken made me dizzy with culinary desire.

Alas, it was not to be.

I had eaten sushi only once before and hadn't liked it much, but we had already arrived at the restaurant, and my tendency to go with the flow, despite the direction it was heading in, stopped me from objecting. We were seated almost immediately, and I perused the small, laminated menu, desperate to find something—anything—that wasn't raw and/or garnished with hot mustard and ginger.

The waiter arrived with two glasses of water and a notepad.

"What would you like?" Michael asked me politely.

"Not sure. What about you?"

"I'm getting this." He pointed to a colorful illustration of raw fish wrapped in seaweed. I felt my stomach heave.

"I think I'm going to pass on the raw fish this time around."

"Don't you like sushi?"

"Oh, sure," I lied. "Doesn't everybody? But I think I'm going to go with the beef negamaki." It wasn't prime rib, I thought, but at least it was cooked.

The waiter, order taken, hurried away.

"So how long have you owned the store?" I asked, wanting to get off the subject of raw fish.

"Me? Own Michael's?" He laughed a little too hard, the idea

seeming to amuse and surprise him at the same time. "No . . . the name thing is just a coincidence. The real Michael spends most of his time playing the horses down in Florida. I just work there."

"Oh," I said, trying to hide my disappointment.

"What do *you* do?" Michael asked, interested.

"Me? Well, right now I work as a kind of waitress at McMullen's."

"A *kind* of waitress?"

The sushi restaurant was small, hot, and crowded so I picked up my menu, which the waiter had left behind, with the hope of generating a breeze. "OK. A *waitress* waitress."

"You want to be an actress?"

"No," I said a little curtly, fanning myself with the menu. "I'm not sure yet what I want to be."

"I'm sorry," he said, slightly stung by my tone. "It's just that most people who work in New York as waiters want to be actors."

"Well, I guess that makes me the exception," I said, sitting a bit straighter in my chair and trying not to appear—as I had started feeling lately—like a twenty-eight-year-old loser.

Michael leaned in toward me. "I know we just met and all," he said without a trace of guile, "but I think you probably *are* an exception."

I couldn't help it. I rolled my eyes.

"OK." He smiled. "So maybe it *does* sound a little lame. But trust me, Isabel, sometimes it takes longer than we'd like to find the right path."

Pretty reassuring words, I thought, for a Chicken Man.

"So," I said, picking up my glass of water and swirling the contents, "do you live in the city?"

"No," said Michael. "I have an apartment in Queens."

"Queens?" My impression of the outer boroughs was derived from the condescending comments hurled by fellow city dwellers. I had never actually met anyone who lived in one of them. "So I guess you take the train to the city?"

"I drive, actually."

"Back and forth? To the city?"

I hadn't meant it to sound like a challenge, but Michael reached into his back pocket as if for a dueling pistol and retrieved his license and registration. I glanced at the license politely. Michael looked pensive in the small photo, his brow slightly furrowed. His attention was focused to the left of the camera, as if, at the last moment, something had caught his eye.

"Ackerman?" I asked. "Is that Jewish?" Born and raised a Jew myself, I had no interest in dating one, finding they rarely left much of an impression.

"My father is Jewish but my mom was Irish Catholic," he answered, pulling apart his wooden chopsticks. "She converted when she married my dad and regretted it every Christmas. You?"

"Yeah . . . I'm Jewish. Not very observant though. My favorite parts are limited to the holidays that include eating my grandmother's brisket and hanging out with my first cousins."

He laughed—an easy laugh that lit up his eyes and revealed a slightly crooked front tooth. I was just about to hand back his license when my eyes fell on the birth date.

I tried to figure the number in my head. "According to this you would be . . ."

"Forty-three in February."

Whoa, I thought. Fifteen years older than me. With his

lightly freckled skin and muscular build, I would have pegged Michael at no more than thirty-five.

The waiter came over to the table with our drinks. I got something that came in an aquarium-size glass garnished with colorful and prodigious amounts of fruit. Michael got a Coke.

"So," I asked, trying to maneuver a sip of my drink while avoiding a poke in the eye from the pineapple, "are you *from* Queens?"

"No. Brooklyn. You?"

"Born and raised in Philadelphia. I came to New York to be a clothing designer. Hasn't worked out quite the way I planned."

"I've found that not much in life does," Michael said, more with delight than resignation. "Anyway, I moved to Queens after my divorce."

"Divorce?"

"Yeah. It's been a few years now. The worst part of it is not getting to see much of my kids."

"Kids?"

I wondered if he noticed that I sounded like an echo.

"Yeah, David and Jordan, fifteen and seventeen."

A moment passed.

"I think that's where you're supposed to say 'fifteen and seventeen?' " he said with a grin.

I guess he noticed.

The main course arrived a few minutes later, and silence descended as Michael, chopsticks flying, disposed of every single one of the beautifully wrapped fish put in front of him. After the waiter cleared the plates, Michael casually reached across the table and took my hand. It swallowed mine, his hand. It was rough and big, the hand of a working man. The kind of hand that doesn't easily let go.

I felt a spark.

"There's something else I'd like to tell you," he said, "and I'm not sure how to start."

My God, I thought, keeping tally of his flaws. There's more? Was he impotant? Did he live with his parents?

Using my free hand, I fished around the remains of my drink for the maraschino cherry.

"I'm a recovering alcoholic," he said. "I haven't had a drink in over seven months, but still, I thought you should know."

I looked at him as if he were the Tooth Fairy. Or perhaps a large Christmas elf. I had certainly heard of alcoholics before, but my exposure had been limited to an old Jack Lemmon movie involving wine and roses. The most my family imbibed was a glass of Manischewitz at Passover. I didn't want to sound unsophisticated, but I was not quite sure what this entailed.

"What does that mean exactly? You can only drink on holidays and special occasions?"

Michael laughed. "Holidays are for amateurs," he said. "For alcoholics it's the other three hundred and fifty-some days that are the problem."

I suddenly felt uncomfortable with the remains of my jumbo-sized mai tai. And even more so about Michael. I retrieved my hand. We finished dinner. I declined a walk.

"Look, Isabel," he said in the taxi as we headed back toward my apartment, "I know I dumped a lot on you tonight. I didn't mean to. There's just something about you that makes me feel . . . I don't know . . . comfortable."

I knew he was waiting for some kind of response, but my mind felt blank. As we wove through traffic back toward the Upper East Side, I sat quietly and watched as the lights of the city leaned in through my open window.

Michael got out of the taxi at the corner and, before I could manage it, came around to open my door. He reached in for my hand at the very moment I decided that, although he was cute and polite and seemed easy to be with, this was certainly not the guy for me. Evidently my head was not in communication with my mouth. "Would you like to come up and see the view?" The words were spoken before I knew I was going to say them.

He smiled at me as if I had just returned his lost puppy.

He kept hold of my hand as we walked toward my building and up the front stoop. He held it up the thirty-two uncarpeted steps and released it only for the climb up the very last flight that led to the entrance at the roof. I caught my breath, unlocked the dead bolt, and propped the heavy door open with one of my kitten-heeled shoes.

From the top of my building you could see the golden spire of a church two blocks away. We walked over to the high wall that ran along the edge and stood side by side, looking out over the glittering city below. On a warm, still night such as this, you could almost imagine yourself in Venice. Only when looking down would you notice that instead of canals, the street was strewn with garbage.

"It's funny," Michael said, looking across the rooftops. "I've seen that church a thousand times before but from up here it looks like a castle in a fairy tale."

"Which one?"

"Oh, I dunno," he said, his gaze remaining on the lights of the city. "The one with the beautiful princess and the divorced guy from Brooklyn?"

I laughed and moved in a little closer, feeling a jolt of electricity as my bare arm grazed his. He turned me toward him, and we stood close enough for me to breathe him in. He smelled sweet, like freshly laundered sheets. He bent his head and gently put his mouth on mine. He kept it there for a minute, a lifetime.

"It tickles," I said squirming, as his lips brushed my neck.

"That's OK," he answered, the words getting tangled in my hair. "It's supposed to tickle."

We began September at a New York Philharmonic concert in Central Park, where, as per tradition, the last performance closed with a fireworks display. Summer was grudgingly giving way to fall, but the night was still warm and balmy. Michael brought an old, fuzzy blanket to sit on and a feast from the store—roasted chicken, duck, and mashed potatoes. We staked our claim among our city neighbors—young and old, lying on sheets and lounging on lawn chairs, playing catch and feeding babies—scrambling for the last unclaimed patch of grass.

The crowd shifted and settled as the air filled with music so rich and sweet it shook the trees. The sky grew dark and filled with stars.

"What do you think?" I asked Michael, stretched out beside me, as the music moved to crescendo and the sky exploded in brilliant shards of light.

He sat up to face me, his eyes locked on mine. I felt a sense of peace come over me that was far removed from the commotion in the park. He kissed me once . . . twice.

"This is nothing," he answered, reaching up to brush a stray piece of hair from my face. "I've been seeing fireworks since the first time I laid eyes on you."

CHAPTER THREE

"Hi," my sister Wendy said brightly. "We're on the Parkway, on the way home from the beach."

"OK," I told her, curled up on my bathroom floor, "but Michael is dead."

Although I had already repeated this phrase what seemed like a thousand times, it still sounded unreal. Evidently Wendy felt the same way.

"WHAT?" she yelled.

I could hear the kids, her two and mine, chattering in the backseat of her SUV. I asked her to give me a little more time to get myself together before bringing them home. I didn't have the strength or the answers yet to face them.

I got up off the floor and picked out a pair of Michael's jeans. I searched through the drawers for his favorite blue polo shirt, the

one that looked so good with his eyes. I decided on a graveside ceremony and, against the wishes of the rabbi, asked for an autopsy.

"An autopsy is against the Jewish religion," he admonished
me, his voice sounding tinny over the phone.

"But I want to know how he died."

"Tradition says no."

I wavered. Even though we were not very observant Jews, I
didn't want to do something that might screw up Michael's chances
in the afterlife. Sensing my hesitation, the rabbi plowed ahead.

"It's a terrible thing that's happened. But what's done is done.
Accept it and move on."

But I couldn't move on. I may never know what happened to
Princess Diana or if there was a second gunman up there on the
grassy knoll. But I needed to know what killed my husband, a man
who watched his diet, took his vitamins, and looked twenty years
younger than his fifty-five years.

"Forget it," I said to the rabbi. "The autopsy's on."

Having never actually experienced it firsthand, I was surprised to realize that shock felt a lot like labor pains, the reality of
the situation coming and going in waves. In between the hysteria
and shallow breathing, I tried to focus on getting things organ-
ized. The medical examiner arrived with an assistant who looked
like he'd rather be elsewhere. They covered Michael's body with
an old quilt, gently placed him onto a stretcher, and carried him
through the building's lobby, painted with faded murals of the
New York City skyline. I watched from my second-floor window
as they slid the stretcher into a waiting van.

I had little time to adjust to the space left by Michael's physical absence. Ivana was soon joined at my apartment by Phoebe

(who took a taxi to Montclair from her job in New York City), my mother (inexplicably nearby for a business meeting), and friends from the neighborhood. Word of my sudden widowhood spread like wildfire, and my small apartment was soon crowded to the point of overflowing. "Does anyone need a drink?" "Everyone have a coaster?" "Hey! Watch out for that stain on the rug!"

Two hours later, Wendy called to say that she and the kids were around the corner. I left my buzzing living room to go out and sit in the hall. My daughters—Jenna, seven, and Sadie, a few weeks past four—bounded out of the elevator and into my lap, laughing and smelling like the ocean, while Wendy hung back with her two boys. Jenna, poised and pale with hair like brown silk and a sprinkling of her father's freckles, immediately sensed something was up.

"What's wrong? Why are you sitting out here?"

I told her simply (simply?) that Daddy had gone to heaven. She looked at me wide-eyed for a moment and then burst into sobs. I'm not quite sure if she knew where heaven was, but she sure as hell understood that it was not at home in front of the TV with her, sharing a contraband pile of Oreos. And so she crumbled. Sadie, as was her habit, followed Jenna's lead, her dark saucer eyes filling with tears. I stood up with some effort and headed back down the hall. Wendy, after bestowing a prodigious hug, trailed a few steps behind with her boys, Max, already taller than me at fourteen, and Eric, quickly gaining, at twelve.

I half led, half carried, my kids back to the apartment, crammed with noise and sympathy. They disappeared into the arms of friends and relatives and, by day's end, emerged years older than the children who had left the beach a few hours before.

Give me strength, I prayed. For my girls. Please give me strength.

The phone began to ring off the hook. An amazing number of people called to "reassure" me that things weren't really so bad.

"Just wait," they murmured, "until the shock wears off." "It'll get worse," said another, "this time next year." Just when I was beginning to think I might be in the clear by the time I hit forty-five, a client shared the good news.

"You should see my best friend's wife," he said sympathetically. "The third year after her husband died she completely fell apart."

How nice it was to have something to look forward to.

The remainder of the day slid past like soft butter, which, along with the other food in my kitchen, I had no desire to consume. Ivana said it was normal, my body's response to shock. My Jewish mother wasn't buying it and kept trying to force-feed me brisket.

As night fell, the majority of mourners returned to their houses and families, shaking off my tragedy like rain from a wet umbrella. But not everyone left. Recognizing the confines of our small two-bedroom apartment, Michael's sons Jordan and David, now grown men of twenty-seven and twenty-nine, rented a Winnebago and parked it in the back lot. Phoebe and my mother made do on opposite sides of the sofa bed, while my neighbor Ida, in Rhode Island for the summer, allowed the overflow to stay at her place next door. My sister Wendy told me that, except for the specter of the large crucifix hanging over the bed, it was really quite comfortable.

Used to being in charge, my mother took command of the situation like a general of his troops. I turned out the light when she said it was time to turn off the light. I slept when she said it was time for us to sleep. The day ran through my head in a continuous loop, and I woke up the next morning asking for very strong pills.

It was December in New York City, and small white lights outlined the trees along Park Avenue like so many diamond-festooned socialites. A few blocks east, I sat hunched over *The New York Times,* searching for a job that didn't require refilling sugar bowls and ketchup bottles. I had written and rewritten my résumé, putting the emphasis by turns on my creativity, my efficiency, and the nimbleness with which I handled a tray. I researched possible employers, spoke to endless headhunters, and made hundreds of cold calls.

It was late Friday. I had just arrived home from a brutal lunch shift during which I had been humiliated by a matching set of designer-clad five-year-olds, only to find another in a long line of rejection letters for a job I was sure I would get. Up to this point, I had been doing well at remaining stoic, a disposition I had been mastering for years.

There had been little room in my childhood for excess emotion. Between my parents' fighting and my sister's moodiness, no one would have noticed anyway. With the exception of a few Campbell Soup commercials, I hadn't cried in years, seeing no upside to the attendant bloodshot eyes and runny nose.

But holding the Xeroxed form letter in my hands, I suddenly felt empty and hopeless. And I broke.

"Hey," Michael said, hearing my stifled sobs as he came through the door to pick me up for a movie. "What's wrong?"

He strode over to the bed where I lay curled up clutching a pillow.

"What's wrong?" I stuttered, embarrassed to be crying and too upset to stop. "My . . . life . . . is . . . a . . . mess." I sat up and reached for the box of tissues on my night table. "I'm tired of being a failure. I'm tired of not knowing what I want to do with my life. But most of all I'm tired of eating breakfast cereal for dinner and listening to my mother tell me to come home and wise the hell up!"

Michael held me close until the sobbing subsided into hiccups, my tears wetting the neck of his T-shirt. Then he whispered something in my ear.

"I love you, Isabel Rosen."

"What?" I asked, pulling away mid-sob.

"I said, 'I love you.' "

I wiped my eyes with the back of my hand and looked him straight in the eye. "But it's been only a couple of months. You can't love me *yet!*"

"Who says?"

"But why? My life is a mess . . . I'm a mess," I wailed, on a roll again.

"You're not a mess. You're beautiful. And believe me, honey, I understand. I'll tell you what they tell us in AA. Just take it one day at a time. And trust that when something is supposed to happen, it will. I know it's hard. Some days it might seem impossible. But then something changes. You make a new friend. You find a job." He paused so I could get another tissue and blow my nose. When I finished, he added, "You meet someone and fall in love."

And, just like that, eyes bloodshot and nose runny, I realized that I loved Michael too.

Michael and I saw each other daily—for a few minutes following my lunch shift, chicken dinner on my roof, a walk in the park. We both loved road trips and jumped into his black, two-door Pontiac Grand Prix at every opportunity. We drove to Woodstock in the winter, stayed at a bed and breakfast, and built igloos in the snow. We went to Jones Beach in the spring and huddled in an old blanket by the shore. He serenaded me with Elvis Presley songs and gave me sixty-minute back rubs. A year later we still came together at the end of every day in the center of my bed, fitting together like two halves of a whole, wrapped around each other like twine.

"I'm not sure what to wear to the interview," I told Michael, scattering clothes all over my bed.

A month before, a socialite had scheduled a soiree at the place where Phoebe and I were still waiting tables. The restaurant's owner thought that if the party was mentioned in the local papers it might bring in more business. I had always had a talent for exaggerating and a problem with talking too much, so I offered to write something up and send it to a couple of editors. When a story appeared a couple of days later in *The New York Times,* my career as a publicist was born. I had spent most of my life left of the spotlight, so having a job that entailed shining a light on others seemed like a natural fit. I had finally found my talent. The only problem was finding someone who would pay me to use it.

"Tell me about the job again," Michael said, trying to find a place to sit amid the piles of clothes, shoes, and faux designer handbags.

"It's a small public relations firm that specializes in fashion and lifestyle clients," I said, pulling on yet another skirt-shirt combo.

The firm was located about twenty blocks from my apartment, situated in the sweet spot between Bergdorf Goodman and Barneys New York. The lobby was a mass of reflective glass and silver, and my image—small, unremarkable, and multiplied a thousand times—stared back at me as I waited for the elevator. I stepped out at the fourteenth floor onto a carpet so plush that its nap almost reached my knees. I hobbled over to the receptionist, an exceedingly thin girl with an exceedingly chic haircut seated at an exceedingly fashionable Phillipe Starck desk, who appeared to be wearing exactly the same outfit as mine—a simple black skirt and a black, long-sleeved crewneck sweater—except that hers, I noted with envy, was not procured at the Limited. When the ringing phone stopped long enough for her to look up, I pounced.

"Hi," I said hurriedly, smiling my most professional smile. "My name is Isabel Rosen and I have a one-thirty interview with Kelly McGrath."

She motioned for me to sit—her wrist bending in the air like the neck of a swan—and I passed the time reading all the latest fashion magazines I couldn't afford to get at home.

A few minutes later Kelly floated into the room wearing an expression of utter serenity. Only when she extended her hand to say hello did I notice, to my relief, that although she was stunning and perfect, her nails were bitten down to her elbows. We retreated into her office, a largish affair that was furnished more sumptuously than my apartment. The air smelled of oranges. I handed her my résumé. She took it and sat, her hair falling over one green eye like a golden blonde curtain.

"We're looking for someone for an entry-level position," she said, her voice emanating from somewhere behind her hair. "I know that you don't have much experience, but I was very impressed by your writing samples."

"I'm fine with entry level," I told her, trying to strike the right balance between professional and I'd-sleep-with-the-building's-security-guard-if-only-they'd-hire-me.

"The pay isn't much," she said, "but there are some perks."

I nodded. I love perks.

"That's great then," Kelly said, closing the file folder on her desk, "but there *is* one last thing. All of our potential hires have to meet with Mrs. Rand." There was something about the way she said "meet with Mrs. Rand" that made my spine tingle.

Kelly stood first and checked her lipstick—a pale shade of pink that perfectly complemented her I-have-a-tan-from-my-winter-vacation-in-Palm-Beach coloring—in the mirror across from her desk. Then she smoothed down her tweed pencil skirt. Even with the deep pile carpet she was at least 5'6".

She led the way down a long hall hung with gilt-framed pages from glossy magazines—product placements featuring the company's array of clients. We came to a closed door. I watched as Kelly took a deep breath before knocking.

A voice boomed from inside. "Come!"

Kelly swung open the door, revealing what to my suburban eyes looked like some fantastical alternate universe. The carpet was zebra; the walls were a delicate shade of pink. The spotless cream-colored sofa, piled high with cushy pillows, was lit on either side with delicate golden sconces. Thousand-dollar handbags fought for floor space with mismatched pairs of Manolos and Jimmy Choos, giving the impression of some kind of bloodless designer battle-field. But the focal point of the massive space was the desk, huge and ornate, and the woman who sat imperiously behind it.

I had never seen anyone like her before, except maybe in some fevered dream brought on by too much takeout Chinese. Her posture was ramrod straight, and her body was almost as slim as her surgically enhanced nose. Her hair was black and contrasted mightily with her taut, pale skin and ruby lips. Ignoring New York's preference for black and more black, she wore a satin blouse of emerald green punctuated with heavy gold cuffs.

She was browsing through what looked like an auction cata-log and waited a moment before looking up. Her laser-sharp eyes focused on Kelly. For once I was grateful not to be the center of attention.

"Where is my tea?" she asked, enunciating each word as though she could taste the letters.

"I'm not sure," said Kelly, clasping her raggedy nails behind her back as if fearing a surprise inspection. "Would you like me to go and check?"

Mrs. Rand shook her head slightly but decisively. Then she did something odd. She picked up a small bell, which sat on a silver tray to the left of her phone. She picked it up—this tiny bell—and shook the thing with all her might, at the same time bellowing at what appeared to be the top of her skinny little lungs.

"Rosa!" she cried to the air in front of her. "Bring me my tea!"

"I'm telling you, Phoebe, it was like something out of a Marx Brothers movie. Here she was one minute, so regal and correct. And the next she's almost standing on her desk like the Hunchback of Notre Dame yelling for her Earl Grey."

Phoebe and I had arranged to meet for a late lunch at Bergdorf's following my interview. It was an indulgence, of course, but Phoebe had hinted earlier that this would be somewhat of an occasion. She had told me that morning that she had some special news to share, which, despite my pitiful begging, she had refused to do over the phone.

"Jeez, you better make sure getting her tea is not part of *your* job description." She slipped a piece of pumpkin muffin into her mouth. "So when do you think you'll hear back?"

"Soon, hopefully. But what's your news? Did you get a part?"

"In a way," she said coyly, wiping a stray crumb from her lips.

"*In a way?* You gonna make me beg, Phoeb?"

"Sorry," she said with a dramatic pause. "It's just that . . . Henry *finally* asked me to marry him!"

"That's great!" I told her, leaning over the small table for a hug.

Phoebe had picked up Henry—along with a toothbrush and some floss—when she had gone to get her teeth bonded six months before. Evidently her career as an actress just couldn't measure up to a handsome guy with a drill.

"He seems nice enough" was Michael's appraisal following our double date a few weeks before. I wasn't so sure. Where Phoebe was bright and effervescent, Henry seemed rather staid and flat. But he treated her well, almost basking in her glow, so, after commenting on his unusually bright smile, I kept my opinions to myself.

"Will you get a ring?" I asked.

"Hmmm. Henry mentioned something about going with a two-carat."

"Wow."

"But then the jeweler found a bigger stone and Henry made the mistake of mentioning it to me."

"Uh-oh."

"Do you know he *actually* asked me the difference between a two-carat stone and two carats and a quarter?"

"Let me guess. A quarter carat?"

"That's what Henry said. And then *I* said, 'Think of it this way. If God told you He could give you a two-carat-size penis or a two-and-*a-quarter*-carat-size penis, which one would *you* go for?' "

"So I gather you'll be getting the two and a quarter."

She shook her head in the affirmative. "Hopefully in a week or so."

"Weird, isn't it?" I said to my friend as the waitress delivered our twenty-dollar salads. "Just a few months ago we had no clue. You were gonna be an actress and I . . ."

". . . you had *bigger* things planned."

I laughed while Phoebe checked her appearance in a piece of shiny silverware.

"Funny," she said, "what happens when you're not paying attention."

CHAPTER FOUR

According to Jewish tradition, Michael's funeral should have been scheduled for the following day. But Michael had died late Wednesday and—the funeral business being somewhat like the TV news business—we had missed the cutoff for a next-day affair. I spent the interim days consuming nothing but tranquilizers and air, while enough party trays and gift baskets piled up in my tiny kitchen to feed half of Newark.

Friday dawned hot and humid. I awoke from a restless sleep, still half drugged from the night before. My head sent a message to my legs, which somehow got garbled around the vicinity of my navel. *What goes?* I asked my unresponsive limbs? In the space of two days I seemed to have lost my toehold in the place that had been most familiar. Everything looked very bright and terribly surreal. From the bent plastic hangers in my clothes closet to the alarm clock standing at attention on my crowded night table, they all seemed to be trying to say something that was slightly out of my range of hearing.

Or perhaps it was just the pills.

Jenna and Sadie, as if in a parallel universe, were playing with Wendy's kids in the back bedroom. It was a beautiful summer day in August and it was time to get dressed for my husband's funeral. *My* husband's funeral. My *husband's* funeral. No matter where I put the emphasis, it just seemed wrong.

What was it I was supposed to be doing?

My mother called in from the other room. "Isabel? Do you need help getting dressed?"

Right . . . that was the assignment. Dressed . . . I had to get dressed.

I stood in front of the mirror. Someone had turned on the television in the living room, and the voices from a *Seinfeld* rerun wafted in to me.

"Maybe if you throw on the black pantsuit no one will notice that you're crazy with grief and totally stoned," Jerry Seinfeld said.

"I don't know," said Kramer, as if peering into my overflowing closet. "Why do you even *have* to wear black? How about the little pink number? Start a trend . . . break new ground!"

I looked at Kramer with a cold stare.

"No pun intended," he quickly replied.

Then Elaine chimed in. "I think you should wear the little black dress," she said, giving me the once-over. "It's not too fancy, won't wrinkle in the limo, and it's *perfect* for any occasion."

I slipped the dress over my head, briefly conscious of how easily it skimmed my hadn't-touched-food-in-forty-eight-hours body.

I was dressing for a funeral. *My husband's funeral.*

I think I might have ended up wearing a hat.

A week after I got hired for my first public relations job, Michael proposed over a corned beef and pastrami sandwich at a New York deli. He didn't have a ring, and he didn't get down on one knee. We had been going out for a year.

"Pass the mustard," I replied when he asked for my hand.

"Pass the mustard? I just asked you to marry me."

"I know. I'm stalling for time," I said, stalling for time.

"Any particular reason?"

"A few," I conceded.

I took a breath and continued ticking the reasons off on my fingers. "An ex-wife. Two kids. Recovering alcoholic. Frankly, honey, I don't know if I can handle it all."

What I didn't include in the litany was my lingering anxiety over the idea of getting married—my fear of failing in the divertissement known as wedded bliss. The specter of my mother and father, guns metaphorically drawn during most of my childhood, continued to haunt me.

Michael stood up and inched his way around our small table. It was dinner time, and the deli was crowded with tourists looking for exotic Jewish foods that they couldn't find back home in Nebraska. He took my hands in his, pulled me to a standing position, and—heedless of the hungry crowd—put his lips on mine. When we broke free a moment later, I took a deep breath and I looked at him.

"That was some kiss," I said, flushed.

"That was more than a kiss."

"You're telling me."

"Seriously, Izzy. That was a declaration."

"What did you declare?"

"That I love you, you idiot." And then quieter, so that I had to lean in to hear him. "And that I want to spend my life with you. Forever."

"Forever's a long time," I said, thinking of how long it had taken me to discover my calling, find a job, meet a nice guy, and finally get my life on track.

"It will be if I have to spend it without you. And no eye-rolling, please. I'm trying to be romantic here."

I blinked.

"It's OK if you're not sure," he said. "I'm not going anywhere. We can just take it one day at a time."

A big white dress. A wedding. Vows. While I had strapped on a pair of size-six Nikes and fled a life of conformity, my younger sister Wendy had embraced it. She went directly from my mother's apartment to her husband Arnie's four-bedroom ranch house, with scarcely a stop for a breath in between. She mastered the art of cooking the summer after saying "I do," redecorated the house in the fall, gave birth to their first child the following year and their second two years after that.

We were sitting in Wendy's large, sunny, kitchen, and I watched as she warmed a bottle for Eric while his older brother Max ran circles around the dinner table. I once again marveled at my sister's crisp efficiency—her brown hair cropped and neat, her freshly pressed shirt tucked tightly into well-fitting jeans, her stainless-steel appliances gleaming.

"You can't keep using Mom and Dad's divorce as an excuse not to be in a relationship," Wendy said when I told her about Michael's proposal.

I had the weekend free and had left Michael busy in New York City with work, AA meetings, and the gym.

"What I can't understand is how you *can't*. Besides, it's not *all* about Mom and Dad."

"Then what?

"Being afraid to make the wrong choice, I guess." I waved a rattle at Eric sitting in his high chair and tried to coax a smile.

"But don't you understand, Iz? You won't know if it's wrong—or right, for that matter—unless you give it a try."

For years I had floundered in a career world unfamiliar to her. But now it was personal, and Wendy, settled down to a life in sub-urbia, felt qualified to give the advice. She tested the baby's bottle on her wrist. Apparently satisfied with the temperature, she swept Eric up from his high chair and popped the bottle into his waiting little mouth.

"Do you love him?" my sister asked simply.

Did I love him? Michael was the first person in my life who made me feel important. He gave me encouragement, a sense of belonging, and unconditional love.

Michael made me feel tall.

"Yes, Wendy. I do love him."

"Then, Isabel," she said, tossing Eric over her shoulder for a burp, "you better not let him get away."

Two months later I awoke to a dozen yellow roses and breakfast in bed.

"Happy birthday, honey," Michael crooned, carrying a plate of scrambled eggs.

And then like a bolt of summer lightning, it suddenly hit me. What exactly was I waiting for? I had been looking for a place where I fit, and Michael had not only helped me find the path, he had strewn it with bacon and the petals of fragrant yellow roses.

"Will you marry me?" I asked as Michael gingerly sat down beside me, a box of Godiva chocolates in his other hand.

"Come again?"

"Will you marry me?"

He feigned confusion, picking at the bow that secured the golden, five-pound box. "I dunno. I thought I was the one who was supposed to ask. And anyway . . . shouldn't you be down on one knee?"

After he ducked the pillow I tossed at his head, Michael leaned over and fished a permanent marker out of the bedside table. On my ring finger he drew a large, emerald-cut diamond, which I later covered with a Band-Aid so it wouldn't come off in the shower.

We were officially engaged.

Michael and I wanted to get married the following fall, somewhere between where his family lived on Long Island and where my family lived in Philadelphia. But much of the area between New York and Philly was swampland—not the most romantic of settings in which to pledge eternal love.

With the help of my mother and sister, Michael and I finally found a suitable place for the reception in a small town on the banks of the Delaware River. The room was beautiful—part of an old historic inn filled with landscape paintings and floor-to-ceiling windows overlooking the river. It was perfect.

Almost.

The room at the inn was not configured to accommodate a hoopa, an aisle, and tables for a hundred and fifty, so we still needed to find somewhere to perform the ceremony. Apparently there were no Jews in town, which meant no synagogues. I checked out every space within ten miles of the inn, but they were either too small, too booked, or too Catholic.

And then there was the problem of commuting.

"Jewish weddings are always held in one place," my mother announced, slicing a banana for my oldest nephew. She had left my handsome, ne'er-do-well father—two daughters in tow—when I was twelve. While he struggled to make the rent, she started an interior design business that expanded three times in four years, managed a staff of twenty, and—barely a shade taller than I—seldom took *no* for an answer. Especially when she was holding a knife.

It was at my mother's suggestion that we meet at Wendy's house to discuss details of the impending event. Since Wendy and her husband Arnie had eloped, the responsibility for making my mother's Martha Stewart walk-down-a-football-field-length-aisle fantasies come true rested solely on my narrow shoulders.

"But they can't find *one* place," said Wendy practically, bouncing Eric on her knee. "And there's no room for an aisle where they're doing the reception."

My mother shook her head dourly. "People will get lost. They'll be late. They won't want to get back into their cars to travel somewhere else."

"Are you kidding?" I gasped. "Our people wandered the desert for forty days and forty nights! This is a lousy half mile!"

Apparently our reasoning made no difference. I could tell my mother was imagining our guests eternally roaming the hills of Bucks County looking for cocktails and pastry-wrapped kosher weenies.

Between not being able to find a place for the ceremony and my mother's insistence that the ceremony and reception be held at one place, Michael and I were ready to follow in Wendy's footsteps and elope. It was right at this juncture that our florist stepped in to suggest the Phillips-Bennett building, a squat little place at the top of a hill overlooking the picturesque town.

"There's a disco ball hanging from the ceiling," I said to the rental agent/unenthusiastic tour guide as I surveyed the room.

"Yeah," he replied. "Cool, isn't it? No extra charge."

There was also no extra charge for the ambulances parked

in front, for when it wasn't being used for special events, the Phillips-Bennett building was the home of the local rescue squad. On the upside, the space had large windows, nice views, and plenty of room for an aisle. I booked it for the second Sunday of the following September. Now if only I could get rid of the disco ball.

My mother learned my little secret three weeks later when she called the place to ask for directions.

"It's a rescue squad!"

"What?" I asked, breathing into the phone.

"That Bennett-Phillips place!"

"Phillips-Bennett."

"Whatever! It's the place where they park the ambulances!"

"Mom, I'm in the middle of a meeting here."

"Isabel! Do you hear what I'm telling you?" my mother yelled. "There was a siren going off when I called! A very *loud* siren."

"But there was no place else," I groaned, feeling very much like a kid caught with her hand in the cookie jar. I looked up to see my boss inching her way over to me.

"You knew?" my mother gasped.

"Of course I knew! There were ambulances parked all over the place. How could I not know?"

The other end of the line was quiet—a bad sign.

"Mom?"

"You just better hope they have no emergencies during the ceremony. 'Cause if they do, you're screwed."

The year flew by in a haze of work and dieting. Despite heavy rain the night before, the morning of my wedding dawned cool and clear; the red maple trees lining the streets of the town almost shone. Michael and I had booked the honeymoon suite at the inn where we were having the reception, and I had gotten access to the room—replete with fireplace, king-size bed, and a lovely view of the river—a couple of hours early.

I had opted out of professional on-site hair and makeup people, preferring to handle things on my own. Phoebe, having since gained possession of her dentist and her two-and-a-quarter-carat diamond, was to be my maid of honor.

"Your dress hikes up a little in the back," she said, adjusting her coffee-colored silk dress.

"No," I said, turning to look at my reflection, "it's me that does."

My gown, a gift from my father, was cut from ivory Duchess satin. It had a fitted off-the-shoulder bodice with a deep-décolleté, which I obsessively tugged so as to avoid spilling out of it. The skirt, which fell to my ankles, exploded in a riot of matching tulle.

"Stop pulling on your dress. It looks fine."

"I thought you said it hikes up."

"That's the back. The front looks fine. But," she added, looking grim, "you don't have any makeup on."

"I do, too!" I replied. "I've got foundation, under-eye cover-up, eyeliner, mascara, and blush."

"That's what I said. You have no makeup on."

Perhaps in part because of her theatrical training, Phoebe possessed near legendary skill at applying cosmetics. In full makeup—as she was at the moment—Phoebe looked like a goddess. I, in the same makeup, looked like a female impersonator. A bad female impersonator.

Phoebe reached into her bag for her Chanel maple-frost eye shadow, but I was too quick for her.

"But it's your wedding day!" she pleaded, fingers tightening around the applicator.

"Exactly. And I want Michael to know that it's me when I walk down the aisle."

"OK. I won't touch the makeup. But what about your *hair*?"

I arrived at the site of my nuptials and entered the room with a slight sense of trepidation. I hadn't seen the place since my previous visit and wasn't sure how well the planned transformation had come off. I needn't have worried. It looked good even for a rescue squad.

A white satin pathway ran between rows of gilded chairs and led to a wrought-iron hoopa, which the florist had woven with late summer flowers. The mauve curtains were secured with lilac-printed tiebacks. Bits of light, reflected from the disco ball, glinted across the polished wood floors.

"It looks beautiful."

I turned to find Jordan, Michael's oldest son, taking in the décor. In the two years since we had met, Jordan had graduated from high school, come out of the closet, and entered college. We had a lot in common: we were both the eldest of two kids, both children of divorce, and we both loved to shop.

"Nice disco ball."

"I couldn't get them to take it down."

"Don't be silly. I think it looks rather glam."

Truth be told, so did Jordan. He had his father's blue eyes and easy smile, and he wore his rented black tuxedo as if he was born to it.

"So says you."

"Seriously, Iz. Everything looks beautiful. Including," he nodded toward me, "the bride." I tried for a curtsy. "And now that you're almost officially my stepmom, I'd like to say thank you."

"For what?"

"For making Dad happy. For helping out with David and me. But mostly for buying my Chanukah gifts at Bergdorf's rather than Stern's."

"Jordan. You're gonna make me cry my makeup off. And then Phoebe will *really* be pissed off."

The preceremony breakfast got off with a bang.

"I thought you said he was coming alone," said my mother between gritted teeth.

"No," I said, trying to appease her, "I said I *thought* he was coming alone."

"Well obviously," she said to me, looking in the direction of my father's attractive date, "you were wrong."

"Look, Mom, he paid for half of the wedding. He can bring a date if he wants."

Although it had been my mother who officially ended their marriage, it was my father who had finally moved on. He would never achieve the business success that my mother had, but a burden had been lifted from his shoulders when he realized that he no longer had to try. The women he dated—and there were many—were happy just to enjoy his company and his dark-haired, movie-star looks. But genial though my father was, it wasn't in his character to back away from a fight. So when my mother threw down the gauntlet in the form of an insult about his date's taste in formal attire, my father responded in kind. The ensuing argument was caught on the videographer's tape for posterity. Wendy, as had been her way since childhood, completely ignored the situation, seemingly engrossed in her husband and a tray of chocolate rugelach. All that was missing, I thought miserably, was a FOX News camera and police tape marking off everyone's territory.

I walked outside to escape for a few minutes, ponder my future, and admire the view. I managed a couple of deep breaths before my father strolled up beside me.

"You look beautiful," he told me, taking me by the hand and spinning me around. "I can't believe my firstborn is old enough to get married. And me still only twenty-five!"

"You and Mom certainly act it."

"Ouch," he said, taking a step back as if avoiding a punch. "But I guess I deserve it."

"You *guess!*"

"Look, Iz, I'm sorry. Really I am. Your Mom and I don't plan on fighting. It just always seems to end up that way."

"You've been saying that since I was ten years old and we got thrown out of Friday's for 'excessive yelling and unruly behavior.' "

"Good salad bar, though."

"I'm not kidding, Dad. What if Michael and I end up like you and Mom?"

"You won't."

"But what if we do?"

He took me carefully by the shoulders, trying to avoid creasing the fabric, and locked his blue-gray eyes onto mine.

"We did the best we could, Isabel. I can only hope that you were smart enough to learn from our mistakes."

"And what if I wasn't?"

"Then you'll cross that bridge when you come to it."

Despite myself, I started to tear up. "And what if I can't?"

He shook his head, refusing to give in to my notions of doom and gloom. "Buck up, Isabel Louise. It's your wedding day. You're healthy, you're kind, and you're beautiful. And you're lucky enough to have found a good man who quite obviously adores you."

Normally I would have disputed the "you're beautiful" and he "quite obviously adores you" statements, but I had always been my father's favorite, and it was his unrelenting affection, even during the moments of parental high drama, that had made my childhood bearable.

"There are no guarantees in this life, honey, but if I taught you nothing else, it was certainly to look on the bright side."

On my way back inside, I bumped into Michael's younger son, David, a tall, lanky high-school senior with an everything-is-groovy vibe.

"The place looks great, Iz. Or should I call you mom?"

I tilted my head up and squinted.

"I think Isabel will be fine, David."

"Cool. Listen . . . do you know if there are any mini hot-dogs left?"

"Not sure about hotdogs but there are probably a few bagels floating around."

"OK. One more thing." He flashed me a grin. "You think I could get 'em to lend me that disco ball for my senior prom?"

Before heading back to the festivities, I stopped in the restroom to check on my makeup. It was there I found my sister in her silk charmeuse designer dress, poised over the toilet bowl, her index finger shoved halfway down her slender throat.

"What are you doing?" I said with some degree of horror.

"Trying to get rid of some stress."

She stood up and sheepishly turned around to face me.

"Looks more like you're trying to get rid of some rugelach." I reached over for a handful of tissues and gently wiped Wendy's face. "I thought you ended this practice when you moved out of the house."

"I did," she said with a weak smile. "Except for special occasions."

"I'm not kidding, Wendy. This is bad."

"And I'm not kidding either, Isabel. If I had to listen to Mom and Dad fight all the time I'd still be wearing a size two."

"It's just one day, Wendy, and a quarter pound of kosher rugelach. And truthfully, if it's all the same to you, I'd prefer not to have a stinky bridesmaid."

Fifteen minutes later, the wedding procession trod lightly across the room to the sound of violins. I took my place at the head of the aisle, watching as my sister and best friend led the way. My father smiled at me and took my arm. My husband-to-be stood across the room, expectant and handsome, the sun shining in his sky-blue eyes. I stood straight and as tall as I could at five-feet nothing and began my walk down the aisle, passing under the disco ball, to meet him.

We toasted with grape juice and shared a kiss. My mom hired a beautiful carriage to take Michael and me to the reception and, even going at horse-and-buggy speed, we managed to pull up to the inn a mere twenty minutes later.

Despite my mother's fears, there were no emergencies and, except for an inebriated second cousin, the rest of the guests managed to find their way.

CHAPTER FIVE

Eschewing the typical black Lincoln Town Car, I drove out to the Long Island cemetery with Wendy and my brother-in-law Arnie in their blue SUV. Jenna and Sadie, wan and quiet in their summer dresses, played as if on autopilot with their cousins in the backseat.

The car pulled up to the front of the chapel. I stepped into the bright sunlight, and people swarmed around me like hungry flies. My father parted the crowd like Galahad, taking my hand gently and leading me to the row of gravestones where my mother quietly joined us.

"You know, baby," my father whispered, "we would do anything in our power to take away the hurt." I nodded dumbly as crowds of people, sweating profusely in their ties and black dresses, jockeyed for position around the grave as if it were a

Rolling Stones concert. The day grew hotter and brighter until the whole lot of mourners resembled nothing more than large, dark smudges against a blinking neon sign. They whispered their condolences and smiled sadly at the kids. I heard a friend who flew in from Florida complain to Wendy that there had been no receiving line. And I . . . I who had planned fashion shows and bridal fairs . . . had neglected to buy a damn sign-in book.

Eventually over sixty of Michael's nearest and dearest—many of whom I recognized and some of whom I didn't—gathered around the hole in the ground to say their farewells. I was stuck in public relations mode, far more familiar to me than the role of grieving widow. I wove between the gravestones, thanking our family and friends for skipping such an obvious beach day to show up at the funeral.

I tried not to imagine my beloved in a box, six feet under, and I didn't want my kids to have to go there at all. At Arnie's suggestion they were safely stowed in the SUV, watching a movie, while the messy business of the burial was at hand.

Back at the gravesite, the rabbi, a man whom Michael had weight-trained on Mondays and Wednesdays, began to speak.

"We are here to mourn the death of Michael Samuel Ackerman." Without thinking, my hand shot up. Surprised, the rabbi nodded in my direction.

"Wrong name," I sputtered. "His name was Michael *Solomon* Ackerman . . . not Samuel. *Solomon.*"

Michael's father, eighty-five and bowed by grief and heat, took my arm and whispered into my ear.

"Isabel, Michael's middle name *was* Samuel."

"*No*. I remember. He had the same name as my grandfather. It's on our marriage certificate. It was Solomon."

Michael's father reached wearily into the pocket of his dark suit and pulled out a green piece of paper. It was Michael's birth certificate, which I needed in order to procure the death certificate.

I took it in my hand, smoothed out the wrinkles, and squinted in the sun.

Born February 2. Michael *Samuel* Ackerman.

So that explained it. The dead man on my living-room floor had not been my husband at all but some lookalike whose middle name was Samuel.

I felt myself beginning to panic.

"Oh my God," I said to my father-in-law. "Does that mean our marriage wasn't legal?"

I glanced toward the SUV. *And what about the kids?* I thought. *Our children are bastards!*

The rabbi was starting to look a little concerned. I whispered again to Michael's father.

"Perhaps we should have asked the rabbi to mention something about Michael's mixed ancestry."

"What mixed ancestry?"

"You know . . . that he was half Irish."

"He wasn't half Irish."

The rabbi put his finger to his parched lips and cleared his throat. Many of the mourners were beginning to molt in the late morning sun, and he reasonably felt it was time to move on.

"Just a minute, please," I said to the rabbi. I turned back to Michael Samuel's father. "What do you mean he wasn't half Irish?

He told me his mom was Irish. I spent fifteen years of my life with a half-Irish man named Michael Solomon. And now you're telling me I didn't?"

I was reeling. I nodded for the rabbi to continue, but thoughts careened wildly around in my head. How could you not know your middle name or heritage? Did Michael dislike the name Samuel and invent a new one? Did he have a thing for green beer and corned beef and cabbage that warranted a change in ancestry?

Perhaps it was true that you never really knew a person.

At the end of a Jewish service the mourners are offered a shovel with which to cover the loved one's casket with dirt. When the spade was offered to me, I took it, feeling Michael's eyes upon me. He had always encouraged me to exercise, and there was no way I was going to wimp out now. I lifted the heavy earth and dropped it into the hole. It fell onto the casket with a hollow plunk. I felt a small sliver of wood from the handle go into my palm. It felt good . . . the way a small pain helps take your mind off a much larger one.

I walked over to the rabbi to thank him for traveling so far from New Jersey to conduct the service. Even through the layers of black clothing I could make out Michael's handiwork. The guy had damn nice muscle tone.

He took my hand in his. "Please, Isabel. If there's ever anything you need, feel free to call me."

I nodded while my mother handed him two twenties.

"It may not seem so now," the rabbi added, wiping sweat from his brow, "but you will, one day again, feel *naches.*"

"I'm sorry, Rabbi, but my Yiddish is a bit rusty. What is *naches*?"

"Joy, Isabel. Joy."

I doubted it.

Service over, the mourners ran gratefully to their air-conditioned vehicles. I climbed back into my sister's SUV, feeling as dry and dead as the ground beneath my feet. My brother-in-law jumped behind the wheel and drove us slowly toward the exit gates.

Five minutes after leaving the cemetery the sky grew dark and it began to rain.

We arrived back at my apartment building near dusk. The sky had cleared, and there was a beautiful breeze blowing through the backyard. The grass was still slightly damp, and the place smelled fragrant with summer and heat and sadness. A few minutes later Jordan and David arrived, trailed by neighbors and friends clutching handfuls of brightly colored balloons. Small pieces of paper appeared. Notes were written and tied to the balloon strings.

"Should we attach Daddy's toothbrush to a balloon and send it up to heaven?" Sadie asked. "How 'bout his pillow?"

I assured her that that wouldn't be necessary.

"I want the blue balloon," croaked Jenna. "It was Daddy's favorite color and I want him to know it's from me."

I took a pen off the wrought-iron picnic table and a little yellow Post-it note. *Dear Michael,* I wrote. *How could you have left me?*

I attached my note to the balloon. I helped Sadie spell *r-e-a-l-l-y s-a-d* and waited helplessly until Jenna—her tears falling onto a seemingly endless pile of tiny pages—was finished. Then I watched as the sun set on another hot August day and fifteen pairs of hands sent messages of love into the late summer sky.

I discovered Montclair, an oasis of parks and houses fourteen miles from Manhattan, while visiting an old friend. Developers had recently pounced on the quarter acre in my backyard in New York City and were tearing up the rosebushes and marigolds in order to erect yet another overpriced apartment building. Apparently the rats and the cockroaches thought it best to relocate to my place during construction.

Michael put cheese from the chicken store into traps that always seemed to go off while we were making love. In spite of his success rate—he disposed of the little corpses several times each day—it quickly became obvious that we were no match for my new roommates. It was time to consider a move.

"I thought you hated growing up in the suburbs," responded Michael when I broached the subject.

"I did. But Montclair is different." Or maybe, by then, it was me who had changed.

"Of course it's different! It's *New Jersey!*"

Like any true New Yorker, Michael believed the Garden State consisted mainly of airports, gas tankers, and mobster hangouts. To tell the truth, having been born and raised just outside of Philadelphia, my conception of the state wasn't that much different.

We drove to Montclair on a crisp, fall day, the trees shining gold and copper in the late afternoon sun. The foliage was the perfect backdrop for streets lined with Colonials plunked next to Tudors plunked next to ranch houses. The neighborhood felt hip and old-fashioned at the same time, the parks scattered with hundred-year-old trees and multiethnic children. It was truly a photo op for the perfect suburban neighborhood and as far removed from the place where I grew up as England was from Idaho.

Michael wavered. A little.

"What about the commute?" he asked, a sensible question for a man who spent at least two hours in his car every day.

"It won't take you any longer to get into the city than it does from Queens," I answered. At least I hoped so.

"Aren't we really close to a nuclear reactor?"

"Not as close as Phoebe and Henry in Westchester."

"Is that supposed to be reassuring?"

There were lots of good reasons to move to Montclair, but it was the local diner and the neighborhood gym that finally clinched the deal. Michael wouldn't move anywhere he couldn't get a good workout and a decent cheeseburger deluxe.

Two years into our marriage and happily ensconced in a spacious apartment, life was humming along for Michael and me. My career as a publicist was on the rise, requiring ten-hour days for the imperious Mrs. Rand. Michael was also putting in long hours at the chicken store, attending regular AA meetings, and doing personal training four mornings a week. As a result of our industriousness, we found ourselves spending less time together than we had when we were dating. All things taken into consideration, it made sense for us to concentrate on our careers and eschew the parent thing.

At least at first.

But over time, almost imperceptibly, my feelings about motherhood changed. I watched, with a bit of envy, the joy Wendy got from Max and Eric. Perhaps, I thought, I might be confusing sentiment with my biological clock. There wasn't a tick, exactly, but there was definitely a hum.

And then I was late for my period.

"Well," I said, dangling the positive, pee-soaked pregnancy test from the tips of my fingers.

It was Sunday morning and Michael, reveling in some rare time off, was sitting on the couch in a T-shirt and sweatpants, reading the sports section of the newspaper.

"Well, what?"

"Well, I'm pregnant."

He put down the paper with a smile. "Of course you're pregnant! What did you expect? We've been having unprotected sex several times a week for over two years!"

"You're not upset?"

To the contrary. He walked over to me and gingerly removed the test from my hand, placing it on the pile of newspapers stacked next to the coffee table. Then he bent down, raised my shirt, and gently kissed my belly.

Michael had spent most of his twenties and thirties working with his dad at a cigar store and luncheonette in New York City, a job that required him to leave his home in Long Island at 3:45 A.M.—before most people had gotten up to go to the bathroom. He was at the store six days a week to greet the coffee-starved masses, consuming a fifth of scotch by lunchtime and still on his feet when the commuters passed by on their way home at five.

By all accounts, Michael was not a mean or obnoxious drinker. He was just mostly absent. He missed a lot of Jordan and David's childhood, and his guilt was visceral. He carried it around in his pocket with his comb. Our child offered him redemption and a second chance at fatherhood, which he grabbed with both hands.

I went into labor at midnight. Seven hours later, my doctor finally gave us the go-ahead to leave for New York City.

The trip into Manhattan took us an hour and a half. My labor pains stopped coming as soon as we got into the car, and I was afraid that when we arrived at the hospital I would be told it was false labor.

Half an hour after arriving, I found myself lying naked from the waist down on a table as my ob/gyn looked on admiringly. And it wasn't just the recent pedicure, an indulgence that Phoebe swore was a must.

"You must have a high tolerance for pain," he said.

"Ah, no, not really," I replied. "Why?"

"Because you're eight centimeters dilated."

By the time Jenna left my womb sixteen hours later, I was spent. I was too weak to hold her so the nurse handed her to Michael. He looked at her wide-eyed.

"What's the matter?" I asked nervously. Did she have ten fingers? Ten toes? It was the first time he had been present at the birth of one of his children, and he looked at her, and me, in awe.

"I almost expected that they'd take her out in pieces and as-semble her on the table."

"No, honey. That would be Mr. Potato Head."

"She's amazing." And at a mere five pounds, eleven ounces, with a head full of dark brown hair, large eyes, and pink lips that turned down slightly at the corners, she was. Jenna and Michael took one look at each other and fell madly in love.

It was the beginning, I hoped, of a wonderful relationship.

For me, having a baby was like watching a great movie. Or secur-ing a great PR placement. My beautiful infant daughter turned out to be even *better* than I had expected. I relished everything from late-night feedings and walks in the park to corny lullabies and pro-jectile vomiting.

Unfortunately, I was relishing most of it alone.

Michael was working fifteen-hour days, six days a week. He had bought a part interest in the chicken store and was working more and making less money than when he had been an em-ployee. He also began having wicked sinus headaches, which proved invulnerable to every treatment but acupuncture.

For as long as I had known Michael, his work was what de-fined him. It also defined our relationship. Besides how hot it should be in the car, work was practically the only thing Michael and I ever argued about. He worked hard. He worked long. And he worked mostly without joy.

"Tommy's taking the week off and I need to cover for him."

"You haven't had a vacation since our honeymoon. Why does Tommy get to take a week off?"

But I didn't have to ask. His business partner was taking advantage, and Michael, perhaps as a result of working with his father all those years before, felt helpless to argue with him.

Meanwhile, my three-month maternity leave was nearing its end, and Mrs. Rand had made it clear there would be no extension. Motherhood had its place, she conceded, but it clearly wasn't in her office, where the hours were dauntless and pumping breast milk between business meetings was as frowned upon as not wearing Prada in a size two.

In the end I succumbed to the charms of my baby daughter and to my burning desire to be a full-time mom. I decided to try freelancing from home, a decision Michael supported, mainly because I handled the bills and he had little idea how much we spent and how much we owed. I worked intermittently, learned how to make a brisket, and tried to find money to balance our checkbook. I joined the stroller brigade at the Short Hills mall but quickly realized I was missing either the Prozac or the patience to enjoy it.

"How do you do it, Wendy?" With nothing else on the schedule that day, Jenna and I went to visit my sister.

"I'll tell you, Iz. It's all about control."

"Control?"

"Yup," Wendy said, enjoying the quiet while her kids were at preschool and Jenna napped. "You have to let go of any pretense of having any."

I couldn't help but chuckle. "That from a former bulimic."

"I'm serious, Isabel. It's all about accepting what you can't change and changing what you can."

"That sounds a lot like AA's serenity prayer."

"It works for overwhelmed moms and former bulimics, too."

"But I'm not sure I can do that."

"Well, I'm here to tell you that there's no other way. Hold on too tight and you'll end up with rope burns. Better to enjoy the little moments, travel through your days like a tourist, and see where the road takes you."

Nine months later and despite my sister's Frommer's Travel Guide advice, the stress of trying to make ends meet and the boredom of trying to keep my apartment clean while single-handedly taking care of an insatiably curious one-year-old was wearing me thin.

"You're never home!" I yelled at Michael, desperate to convey my unhappiness without alarming the neighbors. "You missed her first word! You missed her first steps!"

"I'm trying to earn a living," he answered quietly.

And I wasn't. The rebuke, I thought, hung in the air like so many Christmas lights.

"I don't want to leave Jenna for a sixty-hour-a-week job, Michael. I know what it's like to grow up with parents who are otherwise engaged. I won't do that to my child."

"She's *our* child, Isabel, and I'm doing the best I can."

"But there must be something else you can do . . ."

"I'm forty-eight years old, Izzy. I didn't graduate from college, I'm dyslexic, and I've got bad knees. There ain't a whole lot of career options still open for me."

Perhaps Michael was right. But the guy who wanted a second chance at fatherhood was missing it . . . again.

And then Chanukah arrived. We were celebrating at my mother's impeccably well-decorated apartment where it seemed as if everyone was opening a gift that had been thought out with care and chosen with love.

Michael handed me an unwrapped box of chocolates with the price tag still attached. It wasn't even Godiva, which, though scorned by sophisticated chocolate lovers, had become, along with a back rub and some flowers, our what-to-buy-when-there's-nothing-else-they-want gift.

"I'm sorry," Michael said over the din, "I told Pedro to get Godiva."

"Pedro? You asked Pedro to get this . . . this candy? He barely speaks English! What does he know from Godiva?" I looked at the box with obvious disdain.

"Well . . ."

He was sorry, I could tell he was, and part of me felt that I should accept his apology. But his inattentiveness had gone on far too long.

"Your store is five blocks from the Godiva flagship!" I said, my voice rising in increments. "And there are *eight* days of Chanukah! You couldn't run out after lunch and pick out a box of lousy chocolates?"

I was sad and upset. Not only had I logged in hours at the mall for the family's gifts, but I had also spent weeks wracking my brain for the perfect present to buy Michael. I practically threw it at him—a book on the history of rock and roll that weighed at least forty pounds.

We left Philadelphia at 10:00 P.M. After the nearly five-hour revelry of food and gifts, the silence during the ride home was deafening. Whether it was chillier outside in the softly falling snow or between Michael and me in the car was a toss-up, but by the time we pulled into our parking lot a little after midnight, I had made a decision.

"I can't do this anymore," I said quietly. "I don't want to be with someone who has no time for me. And I don't want our daughter to be an afterthought."

Michael said nothing. I paused and took a breath. Perhaps I was emboldened by the spiked eggnog. "It's us or the job."

This wasn't a new line for Michael. He had heard the same thing years before from his first wife. I was hoping that this time the outcome would be different. But his lack of a response was hardly encouraging.

He parked the car, unloaded the gifts, and carried Jenna upstairs to her crib. I took a shower and wearily climbed into bed.

New Year's Day came and went. Despite my fevered ultimatum, things between Michael and me did not improve. On the contrary, he was putting in even more time at the store than he had before the holidays. I had resolved early on that I would never subject my child to the constant fighting I had witnessed between my parents, so Michael and I just didn't talk at all.

"I know how you feel," Phoebe said sympathetically. "But look on the bright side—at least you have Jenna to keep you company."

It was a warm day in early spring, and Jenna and I had taken a road trip to Westchester. Phoebe, after a short stab at retirement, had gotten a job as an assistant talk-show producer and was commuting back and forth to the city every day. We sat in her huge backyard, drinking fresh-squeezed orange juice and soaking up the afternoon sun while Jenna patiently stacked and then unstacked a pile of blocks on the grass nearby. My daughter had grown into a happy child with a ready smile and an independent nature. Most days I could hardly believe I had helped create a thing of such beauty.

"Any luck on the pregnancy front?" I asked Phoebe.

"No. And there's not likely to be unless I start sleeping with the UPS guy. Henry's never home. If it's not a dental convention then it's some kind of dental emergency."

"Wow. Who'd have thought there'd be so much decay in Westchester?"

"I'm telling you, Izzy. Sometimes I wish for a bad cavity just so he'll make a house call."

I thought back fondly to when Michael used to deliver. Those days, it appeared, had long ago passed.

A few weeks after receiving a credit card bill with an all-new high, I got a call from a headhunter about a job at Goldman & Partners. They offered me a three-day-a week position with a vice president's title and a regular salary. But they had one requirement: I had to work out of their office in New York City. It would mean getting child care. It would mean leaving Jenna.

"Take the job," said Phoebe over an expense-account lunch.

"Why did you?" I asked, curious. If anything, Phoebe seemed born to the role of a doctor's wife.

"I had to," she explained. "Between the cars and the beach house and the motorcycles, Henry was spending money faster than he was making it."

"So it was about the money?"

"Partly. It was more about the identity."

I looked at her curiously. "What do you mean?"

"I mean," she said, throwing up her hands, "Henry got me a license plate for my last birthday."

"A license plate? Did it come attached to a car?"

"Yes, it did," she said, trying to suppress a little smile. "But that's not the point."

"It isn't?"

"OK, so the car was nice. But it was the plate that got me." Phoebe fished a pen out of her handbag, wrote something down on a napkin, and then shoved it over to me. Written out was *H-N-R-Y-S-W-F-E.*

"Oh my God," I laughed, the light dawning. "Henry's *wife?*"

Phoebe began tapping the pen against her water glass. "I spent four years at college, two at the top of my class. I supported myself for four years in the city. I starred in an off-off-Broadway show. Shit, I even played a slutty intern once on *General Hospital!*"

"I remember that."

"And now," she said, "incredulous, in what could be the most productive years of my life, my persona—my very *being*—has been summed up by my husband on a lousy license plate that says *Henry's Wife!* I think not, my friend. I think not." She put the pen back in her bag and closed it with a snap.

"So what'd you do? Take back the car?"

"Don't be ridiculous!" Phoebe said. "I called my friend at NBC and told her I needed a job."

"But what about having a baby?"

"I'll cross that bridge if, God willing, I ever come to it. But I'll tell you something: the way things were going, if Henry and I *did* have a kid, her vocabulary and social life would have been better than mine. I needed some outside stimulation, Iz. And I'm talking besides my vibrator."

"I dunno, Phoeb. I feel so guilty, leaving Jenna."

"Get over it, Isabel. Besides, what you want is an urban myth, kind of like the G-spot and multiple orgasms."

"Really? And what is it you think I want?"

"To have it all, baby," Phoebe said, gleefully scooping up the last of her caramel soufflé. "To have it all."

In anticipation of Michael returning home that night, I planted myself on the living-room sofa and hid the remote beneath some cushions. I gave him a few minutes to relax and grab some Oreos and milk before getting to the point.

"I want to take the job," I told him.

He sat down at the other end of the sofa with his milk and stacked the cookies on the coffee table in front of him. "What about Jenna?"

"Ivana said she'd be happy to watch her."

"What about Austin?"

"What about him?" Ivana's son was a few months older than Jenna and, fortunately for all of us, they adored each other.

"You don't think it'll be too much for her to handle?" asked Michael, unscrewing the top of his cookie.

"I think she'll be fine. Besides, she lives in the building so commuting won't be an issue. And if it doesn't work, we can make other arrangements."

"You really want to do this, don't you?"

"Yes, Michael," I said, wiping a bit of crumb from his mouth. "I really, really do."

CHAPTER SIX

Since Saturday is the Sabbath and all good Jews are supposed to be in a synagogue, shivah resumed at our apartment on Sunday. If it weren't for the fact that Michael was dead, it would have been one hell of a house party.

The fun began early when two old friends, unable to make the funeral, drove up from Philadelphia to help me grieve. There were hugs and kisses and copious reminiscing about the good old days when a tragedy meant you couldn't get a date for New Year's Eve. There was also some curiosity, on my sister Wendy's part, about where the hell Annie, once flat-chested, and Michelle, a small C cup at most, had found two such extraordinarily large pairs of knockers.

I was sitting on the couch in the living room numb and mostly stoned, when I realized my sister and two friends had disappeared. I decided to take advantage of their absence and headed to my bedroom to lie down. I pushed open the door just in time to see a wall of flesh advancing in my direction. For a second I thought I should duck. Wendy was looking toward Annie and Michelle with the kind of awe usually reserved for well-built men and chocolate-covered rugelach. There they stood—two of my oldest friends—topless in my small bedroom, sporting matching sets of double D's.

Wendy reached out a tentative hand in the direction of Annie's left boob.

"Can I touch it?"

Under normal circumstances I might have been first in line to cop a feel, but whatever these circumstances were, "normal" did not adequately describe them. Even *before* I saw the boobs I wanted a drink. Now I needed a double.

I quickly left the room and walked to where my kitchen used to be. In its place I found a catering hall. In all my years of living in that apartment I had never seen so much food in there. A big pot of coffee was brewing. I had no idea where the pot came from, but there it was. Brewing. There was a brisket in the oven, Chinese food on the stove, and a dessert plate on top of the refrigerator. There were baskets and tins, fresh fruit, dried fruit, and nuts. I headed straight for the scotch.

My mom was squeezed between bottles of soda and bags of ice when I walked in. "Hi, honey," she said tenderly. "What can I get you?"

But what I wanted was not in the kitchen. Or in the apartment, for that matter. What I wanted now lay in a cemetery somewhere on the outskirts of Long Island.

"Come on, honey," my mother said, grabbing a paper plate heaped with food. "It's been two days. You have to eat *something.*"

Shivah passed in a blur of food, conversation, and Xanax. Late the second afternoon, I answered a knock at the door to find some of Michael's employees from the chicken store.

They brought food, naturally.

I took one of the trays and led the man carrying a second one into the kitchen. He appeared to be in his seventies and was wearing a yarmulke that sat crookedly on his head. He told me that he was sorry for my loss, liked Michael very much, and would miss working with him at the store. He took a bagel and cream cheese, and we walked back into the living room, where we sat with our knees touching on the sofa. Then he took a breath.

"You know of course about the period of mourning?"

I said I believed it was a year.

"*Oh, no,*" he responded, taking a bite of his bagel. "In the Jewish religion a wife's period of mourning for her husband lasts just thirty days after shivah is over."

I thought I must have heard him wrong.

"You mean thirty *months,*" I responded patiently.

"No. I mean thirty *days.*"

Thirty days to mourn a man I had been with for twelve years? Thirty days to sort through his clothes? Thirty days to get used to being in our bed without his arms wrapped around me? Thirty days of sitting at a dining-room table now set for three? Hell! I thought. Eight times out of the year, thirty days isn't even a month!

The man put his hand on mine and smiled kindly.

But I'm weak, I wanted to say. What if I'm not ready to put down the box of Kleenex, throw on some makeup, and get a date? I knew that life was moving faster than in the old days, but this seemed ridiculous. Perhaps a stronger woman would be ready for dinner and a movie a month after her husband's funeral. For me, it took almost too much of an effort to breathe.

I leaned into him. "What happens then?" I asked. "What happens after the thirty days?"

"Well," he replied, finishing his bagel, "then you start looking for a new husband."

I started my new job on a Tuesday in July. I got dressed in clothes that weren't mostly spandex, put on actual makeup, and—sans spit-up and leaky breast milk—felt vaguely like an attractive woman again. Michael was long gone—he rose most mornings at five to go to the gym—but I spent some time with Jenna before dropping her at Ivana's and boarding the bus that would take me to New York City.

I was Vice President of the Fashion Division—I saw the title in capital letters in my head—and my office had a window, a framed Matisse poster, and a plastic plant. My coworkers were young, funny, and welcoming, and, as much as I missed being at home with my daughter, the regular paycheck and medical insurance helped to ease the pain.

During my second week at work I was scheduled to meet with one of my new clients, the vice president of corporate communications for a national fashion retailer. This was my biggest account, and I was giddy with my new power, kitten heels, and manicure.

The meeting took place in the large and stylish conference room at our offices. After making a selection from a profusion of baked goods and soft drinks, I took a seat at the far side of the wood-veneered conference table, next to Richard, a cute gay guy with great taste and a killer sense of humor who was also my new assistant. I had just taken a bite of my blueberry muffin when *he* stepped into the room. He was tall and lean with fair skin. He had dark brown hair and bottomless brown eyes, and heat came off him like sweat off a long-distance runner. He wore tortoiseshell rimmed glasses that gave him the air of an intellectual. He nodded to Richard, who stood. Then he walked over to where I sat and offered me his hand.

"Hi, I'm Chris Bowman. Welcome to the team."

I smiled. My greatest wish at that moment—more than slimmer hips or world peace—was that I didn't have any stray blueberries stuck between my teeth.

He looked me straight in the eye, and I felt a jolt of electricity shoot through my torso and down my legs to my newly polished toenails. I took his hand with a mixture of confidence and utter lust. I spent the remainder of the meeting hoping he hadn't noticed.

From that first meeting, Chris and I talked almost daily. I told him I was married. He told me he was not. Nevertheless, work conversations about press releases and media lists soon devolved into talk about politics, religion, and family.

"My mother's a pastor in Vermont," he told me.

"So you didn't go into the family business, huh?" I leaned

back into my chair, his voice buried in my ear, and pretended, for the sake of anyone who might pass by, that I was taking notes.

"In a way. My father runs a dairy farm and spends a lot of time shoveling shit."

I laughed. "It's not a bad metaphor."

"Are you kidding? That's being kind. In my mother's eyes, publicists are the Devil's handmaidens and are more responsible for the misery in the world than lawyers are."

"Wow. That's rough. Where does that leave you?"

"Right now it leaves me in New York City with an expense account and a great apartment, doing a job that I love."

"Me, too. It's just . . ."

"What?"

"I feel guilty about Jenna. Not being there for her." I fixed on the bouncing lights of my computer's screen saver.

"Trust me, Isabel, you're doing what you have to. And like I tell my mom, there will be plenty of time to repent later."

I thought about that. About repenting. When the conversations between Chris and me went on longer than they had to, I reasoned that it was business. And being on good terms with an important client *was* good business.

Despite my attraction, I had no plans to embark on an affair. Chris's attentions were good for my ego, but I was married with a child and I didn't plan to let things go further than a casual flirtation.

But that didn't mean I couldn't think about it.

Summer was at its peak, but the heat did nothing to ease the chill between Michael and me. But the dozen pink roses I found on my office desk one Monday morning seemed like the start of a possible thaw. The flowers didn't make everything all right again. I had been busy the previous week on a new product launch, and Michael had promised and then neglected to pick up the slack, but the flowers were definitely a step in the right direction.

I tore open the note while dialing Michael's work number, only to find that the note and the flowers weren't from him. The card read, "Congratulations to my favorite publicist on a successful launch." It was signed "Your Grateful Client."

I hung up the phone. And then I picked up the receiver and dialed again.

"Thanks for the roses," I said when Chris came on the line. I was doodling to control my sudden nervousness. "They're beautiful and you shouldn't have."

"Oh, stop it. You did a great job last week . . . above and beyond."

"I don't know about that."

"Listen, it's crazy here, but I want to get together to talk about next steps."

"Next steps?" My mind wandered . . . where did one go after flirting and flowers?

"Yeah, the national launch went so well, we're thinking about doing something regional. Maybe a media tour in some of the larger markets."

"Sounds good," I said, trying not to sound disappointed that his suggestion was business-related. "What works for you?"

"Hmmm. Today is shot. I've got meetings all day tomorrow and the day after that. Hey, you want to meet late Wednesday?

I'm going to be at the Four Seasons for the new accessories presentation. How about we meet there?"

"The Four Seasons? Yeah, I guess that's OK. What time?"

It was work, I said to no one in particular. I'd be on the clock, earning a living, towing the line. And even if it wasn't, meeting with an attractive client in the lobby of a five-star hotel felt like justified revenge for my husband's continuing disregard.

Michael was planning to go to Westchester on Wednesday to meet a potential investor, so I asked Ivana to stay late until one of us returned home.

The day dragged by so slowly I thought for sure my watch had broken. Two hours before my assignation, I reapplied my makeup. An hour before, I fluffed up my hair. At 3:30, I grabbed some papers and told my staff that I was off to a meeting. At 3:45 I was standing in front of the elevator, and at 3:50 I was running the few blocks to get to the hotel on time, stopping to remind myself that it was just a business meeting and besides, I didn't want to cause any underarm sweating.

Chris was waiting for me in the lobby. My shoes tapping against the marble floors served to disguise the pounding that came from the general direction of my chest. Client or no client, with his brooding profile and thatch of dark hair, the man was just plain gorgeous.

"I've been in a meeting all damn day," he said, casually throwing an arm around my shoulders, "and I, dear Isabel, could use a drink."

A drink. Well, I reasoned, lots of people drink while they conduct business. I'd seen several movies where Rock Hudson and Tony Randall did it all the time.

We moved toward the crowded bar area. Only in New York City could people so tightly packed together still manage to look so entitled. Chris snagged a table off the main drag. We sat across from each other. A pianist played absentmindedly in the next room. We ordered two glasses of chardonnay, and when they arrived at the table, Chris held his up high.

"To you, dear Isabel. To a successful product launch. To a happy vice president. And to upcoming coverage in *The Wall Street Journal, USA Today*, and *The New York Times*."

We drank. I was more used to sharing Juicy Juice with Jenna, and the wine tasted bitter on my tongue.

"So what do you think about Philadelphia, Chicago, LA, Washington, and Boston?"

I pulled out my notes, careful not to upset the plate of crackers and olives. "Sounds good to me. But I want to take a look at the media lists before committing, and we have to be careful with the timing."

"Agreed."

"Speaking of timing," Chris asked casually, "how are things at home? I'm asking as a friend, Iz. Have things between you and Michael gotten any better?"

"No. They haven't." I shuffled some papers, head down. I could feel myself flush, not exactly standard business practice.

"We don't have to talk about it if you'd rather not."

"It's OK," I said, taking a breath and looking back up at him. "It's just hard . . . he's never home."

Chris casually put a hand on mine and peered at me over the rims of his glasses. "I'm sure it's not because he doesn't want to be."

"Come on," I responded, somewhat incredulously.

Chris shrugged his shoulders. "A man's gotta earn a living, Iz. I'm single and childless and even I understand that." He didn't say anything snide or call Michael a jerk. Although it would have been fine with me if he had.

We ordered blini appetizers and a second round of drinks. It was then that Chris put his cards, such as they were, on the table next to the olives.

"I don't want you to think that I make a habit of flirting with married women. Especially married women who work with me."

"Is that what you're doing?"

He smiled. "I guess I need to brush up if you're not sure."

"Yeah . . . I was pretty sure." I shifted in my seat and crossed my legs. They were short, my legs. But with the slight bit of golden tan, I had to admit they looked pretty good.

"I know you've been having a tough time of it lately, and I don't want you to think I'd take advantage of that. It's just that . . . well . . . I wanted you to know that if you need a shoulder to cry on, I'd be happy to provide it."

"A shoulder to cry on? Is that what they're calling it these days?"

I was flattered, but I didn't delude myself into believing that Chris hadn't made the very same sales pitch a hundred times before.

"Discreetly," he added, popping a blini into his mouth. "Of course."

"Of course."

When Chris excused himself to use the restroom, I ate an

olive and checked my lipstick. I *did* need a shoulder to cry on. Who would deny me that? I worked hard, I was a good mom, and my husband didn't appreciate me. What harm would a discreet roll in the hay do? If necessary, I thought, I could do as Chris suggested and repent later.

I squared my shoulders and switched off my cell phone.

I arrived at the bus station two hours later, hopped on the 33, and headed for home. I found a seat toward the back and settled in, too distracted to read, too wired to sit still. I pulled my cell phone from my bag and switched it back on, even though using it on the bus was not allowed. The phone blinked at me in rebuke; there were two messages from Michael and three from Ivana. I slumped down a little in my seat and dialed voicemail, but before it could connect, a call came through.

"*Where have you been?*" Ivana asked, sounding slightly frantic.

"A business meeting."

"At this hour?"

"Yes, at this hour," I replied, a little more snappy than necessary. "Why?"

"I've been trying to reach you all afternoon. Jenna woke up from her nap with a really high fever."

I sat back up.

"What!"

"I tried to call you earlier, but your phone must have been turned off. I finally got Michael but . . ."

"Shhhhhh," said a fellow passenger.

I looked over. There it was, sitting like a bag of chips on the seat next to me. Guilt.

"Tell me," I said to Ivana, heedless of the dirty looks. "What's going on?"

"She woke up so pale and hot. I finally reached Michael, but he said he was at least an hour away so I left Austin with Ida and quick took Jenna to the doctor."

"And?"

"And they said they thought she might have . . . what's it called?"

"I don't know, Ivana," I said, my voice rising. "What's it called?"

"You know . . . something in the throat." When Ivana got excited, her grasp of English, her third language after Serbian and French, became a bit tenuous.

"An infection? Tonsils? Strep?"

"That's it. Strep."

"Is Jenna with you?" I asked her.

"No. Michael came back a little while ago and got her."

I thanked Ivana, mentally urging the bus to go faster. I hung up and called home. The phone rang but no one answered. It was after 8:00 P.M. My daughter was sick. Where could they be?

Dark thoughts ran through my head as the bus inched along toward home. Was it possible to be punished for something you only fantasized about doing? Didn't you get credit for being strong and doing the right thing? Two hours of fully clothed conversation didn't constitute a sin. Did it? Chris had invited me back to his apartment, and I declined. He had offered to get a room at the hotel, and I turned him down. I missed my daughter. I loved my husband.

I burst through the door thirty minutes later, panicked and out of breath, to find Jenna curled up in Michael's arms in the rocking chair in her bedroom, both of them looking content and fast asleep.

Michael must have sensed me there. He woke up, checked his grip on Jenna, and squinted at me in the dim glow of the Mickey Mouse night-light.

"I talked to Ivana," I said.

He nodded. "Jenna's going to be OK. Her temperature went to 104 but it broke about an hour ago. The doctor said to keep a close eye on her. They'll have the strep culture back in the morning."

I felt my knees beginning to buckle and sunk relieved onto the floor.

"I didn't know," I told him, my voice plaintive and seeking forgiveness.

"Of course you didn't," he said.

"I thought you were at a meeting with a potential partner in Westchester," I said.

"I was. But Ivana called and said that Jenna needed me."

Michael stood up and deposited Jenna gently into her crib. Then he took my hands and pulled me into a standing position, our bodies close.

"I know you've been angry with me, Izzy, and I understand why. But please believe that I'm trying. The truth is, there's nothing more important in this world to me than you, Jenna,

Jordan, and David. Contrary to what you might think, I'll always be there when you need me. Always."

I had meant it when I told Michael it was us or the chicken store. I had meant it when I told him I didn't want Jenna and me to come second after his job. But when we got into bed that night, we reached for each other and held on especially tight. Before he left for work the next morning, he kissed my hair and whispered that he loved me. So I cut him some slack about his hours. I handed responsibility for Chris's account over to a coworker, and the daily phone calls stopped. In return, Michael came home early two nights a week and bought me a box of Godiva.

Perhaps it *was* a myth that we could have it all. But in those moments watching my husband with our daughter, I realized that I had more than enough.

CHAPTER SEVEN

Day four following the funeral dawned with the knowledge that even though my husband was dead, my kids still needed clean underwear.

When Michael and I first began living together, I had the job of doing the laundry, but Michael so hated the way I folded his jeans that sometime in year three he begged to take over. Now, less than a week after his death, a mountain of dirty clothes appeared before me, clearly oblivious and indifferent to my loss. I had no choice but to wash, dry, and fluff. Three hours after descending to the basement, the girls playing with Austin at Ivana's, I hauled the hamper back upstairs to the girls' room and began to fold.

Out of the basket and onto the bed. The sweatpants Michael wore to the gym. A pair of boxer shorts with stars that glowed in the dark. T-shirts that Michael had bought the kids the summer before at the Third Avenue Street Fair.

I folded the clothing into neat piles on Jenna's cheerful pink and white comforter while my thoughts careened wildly around the room.

This is now the sweater of a fatherless child.

Can you give used Jockey shorts to Goodwill? Or is that kind of creepy?

Should I still fold Michael's jeans even though I know he'll no longer be wearing them?

As if to mock my mood, the sun shone brightly through the gaily curtained window. And then the floor disappeared from beneath my feet, and I was struck by a feeling of sadness and loss that was simply too overwhelming to bear.

Living the life of a widow with two children was a job for a strong woman, someone with courage and grit. I was a middle-class Jewish girl who didn't know how to cook or sew or date. True, in times of stress I'd been known to channel Katharine Hepburn, but I didn't have the height or the stamina to carry that off long-term.

It would be easier, so much easier, I suddenly thought, just to die.

I considered the idea. The strongest pills in my medicine cabinet—aside from copious amounts of sedatives—were extra-strength Tylenol. Guns and knives were messy and painful and therefore out of the question. Bounteous bushes grew beneath my windows, which excluded jumping as a reliable option. Pills would be the best way, really. But what kind and how many? Could I order them online and have them shipped from Canada?

What I needed was a book on how to kill yourself. I was sure I could probably find something on Amazon. I would take the pills, close my eyes, and be with Michael again. After all, I had had a good life. I had traveled. Been in love. Had two great kids.

Ah . . . the kids.

I picked up a tiny pair of Dora the Explorer underwear. I couldn't leave my girls. And since I knew in my heart that no matter how much I might want to take my life I wouldn't, I put the thought away in a drawer, along with Sadie's clean underwear.

In the three years since giving birth to Jenna, I had loosened my grasp on all-things-Manhattan and reluctantly found a local ob/gyn. There were, of course, perks. Instead of driving an hour into the city to give birth, Michael and I picked up snacks, had the car washed, and took a leisurely drive to Mountainside Hospital, located just around the corner.

Our second daughter was born right before midnight.

Sadie was a lovely baby with big brown eyes, a ready smile, and an easy disposition, but it quickly became obvious that she lacked both the serenity and the coordination of her older sister. When Goldman & Partners declined to give me maternity leave (I was technically a part-time employee), I decided to try freelancing again, giving myself a front row seat for the ensuing action at home. And I *do* mean action.

At the age of two and a half, Sadie jumped out of a bathtub and ran naked—her preferred mode of dress—through the living room. When Michael chased her back, she leapt back into the tub and bashed her head on the spigot, requiring five stitches above her left eyebrow. Later, she proudly told anyone who might be interested that she didn't even cry.

She celebrated her third birthday by falling off the monkey bars at the playground. She was a mere two *inches* above the ground but still managed to fracture her wrist. We didn't even realize the extent of her injury until the following day because she never complained that it hurt.

If Sadie's distinction lay in seeing how many bones she could break before her fourth birthday, Jenna's skill lay more in trying to create a masterpiece by the time she entered third grade. She loved to draw and paint, which she did, with great gusto and no newspaper, all over our butcher-block dining-room table. I finally decided to stop trying to scrape off the remains of her projects and simply attribute the décor to early Jackson Pollock.

July, so far, had been hot. Sadie's fourth birthday party was a couple of weeks away, and Jenna had just finished up a week at the neighborhood art camp. With Michael stuck at the store that Saturday, the girls and I decided to take a drive. We ended up in Phoebe's backyard, the two of us relaxing on expensive chaises and drinking iced tea, while Jenna and Sadie splashed around in a borrowed, purple plastic kiddy pool.

"Still no luck with the baby thing, huh?" I asked, lazily stirring the ice tea with a sippy straw. "Have you thought about trying something else?"

"What else is there? The hormones they gave me for the in-vitro made me crazy, I don't want to use a surrogate, and Henry doesn't want to adopt." Phoebe shrugged her shoulders in resignation. She tried to act casual, but I knew how much she wanted kids.

I smiled a sympathetic smile.

"Hey," Phoebe asked, flipping through a magazine. "Have you thought of getting your teeth whitened?"

"How did we get from you not being able to get pregnant to the state of my teeth?" I reached for my handbag in search of a hand mirror so that I could take a look.

"We did a story on it a couple of weeks ago."

Phoebe had quickly risen through the ranks of trash talk and now claimed the title of senior producer at a national show.

"You did something on teeth whitening? That sounds kind of lame."

"Actually, the title of the segment was 'Cosmetic Surgery for Kids: How Young Is Too Young?' "

"Sounds like another Emmy winner to me."

"Ha ha. I'm telling you, Iz, it makes a huge difference."

Phoebe flashed hers for effect. She may have been a dozen years older than when we first met, but the years had been very kind.

"That's what you said about Botox," I said.

"And I was right."

"They're shooting the same toxin that causes food poisoning inches from your brain!"

Phoebe gave me one of her you-are-so-uninformed hand waves.

"So forget about Botox," she said. "But you *should* do your teeth."

I studied myself in the mirror.

"It's been great for Henry's practice; everyone in Westchester wants a Farrah Fawcett smile."

"From what I hear Farrah's not using it much lately."

"Poor Farrah." Phoebe picked up a cookie and nibbled at the edges. "So. How about you? Are you a happy enchilada?"

"Very happy."

Michael had found a new working partner the summer before, allowing him to cut down his hours and spend more time at home. Business was good and chickens were flying out of the store like . . . well, chickens.

"Work is great," I told Phoebe. "I have a couple of retainer accounts that help pay the mortgage but leave me time to spend with the girls."

"Sounds perfect," said Phoebe, pointing her face toward the sun.

"Not perfect, but pretty damn good." I put the mirror back in my handbag and tossed it on the ground. "Considering where we were about a dozen years ago, I'd say we've netted out pretty well."

"You should spit when you say that," said Phoebe quickly. "Keeps away the Evil Eye."

I looked around at her polished deck and her professionally manicured lawn. "Really?"

"OK, maybe not," she said with her perfect smile. "But at the very least, Isabel, you should have your teeth whitened."

The following month, on a lark, Michael and I scheduled appointments with the dentist. Mine was for Wednesday, a hot afternoon in August. Michael had a headache when I left. When I got home,

I thought, we would probably share a Caesar salad in front of the TV while watching a favorite *Law and Order* rerun. He might put his head in my lap, and I'd massage his temples until the pain went away. I would think about how much we had been through together, how lucky we were to have two beautiful daughters, and marvel at how generally well life was going.

If only I had spit.

CHAPTER EIGHT

"Where do they go to the bathroom?" asked Sadie. Unlike Jenna, who remained shell-shocked following her father's death, it hadn't taken my younger daughter long to get into a party mood. I was trying to organize dinner—cook was too strong a word—while Sadie whirled around my legs like a determined little top.

"Do they have beds up in heaven or sleeping bags? Where do they go when it rains?" And finally, "Now that Daddy's not down here anymore can we get a dog?"

"No, Sadie. We can't." I took four plates out of the cabinet. And then I put one back.

"But you said we couldn't get a dog 'cause of Daddy's allergies."

"That was true, honey, but even if Daddy's allergies weren't an issue . . ."

"What's an 'issue'?"

"A problem. Even if Daddy's allergies weren't a problem, they still don't allow dogs in the building."

"*Please.*" After the last two days, the look of pleading on her face was almost enough to kill me.

"I'm sorry, honey," I told her, dropping frozen ravioli into a steaming pot. "We can't get a dog."

"OK." She sighed, perhaps sensing her mom was on the verge of a nervous breakdown. "How about a hamster?"

I was sitting at my desk, staring blankly at a press release on my computer screen, when Ivana called.

"Look, Izzy, I'm not really sure how to ask you this . . . but what do you think about psychics?"

"Psychics?"

"Yeah, you know. People who talk to dead people."

I was never a very religious person, but I grew up comfortable with the idea of alternative ideologies. I believed in astrology, the possibility of life on other planets, and the transformative powers of shopping. I did, however, draw the line at fortune-tellers.

I may have been open-minded. I wasn't insane.

"I dunno. Why?"

"I have this friend Rebecca. She called me yesterday, kind of upset. She told me something bad had happened to someone I knew and right away I thought of Michael. I told Rebecca that we thought it was a heart attack—and she said *no,* that's not what happened. Freaked the hell out of me, but I thought maybe I should mention it. She said she'd be happy to talk to you, if you want."

Ivana was unsure of Rebecca's psychic claims—what normal person wouldn't be? But Rebecca, a telepathic carpool mom who lived on the West Coast and had never met me or Michael, seemed to have information about my husband's death that she really had no way of knowing.

I was still waiting to hear back from the medical examiner—a process I was told could take a couple of weeks—and I didn't know for sure *what* had killed Michael. The fact that a stranger who lived over two thousand miles away had the scoop before I did disconcerted me. But then again, I reasoned, if Rebecca could put me in touch with Michael, it was certainly worth a try.

I called and booked the first available appointment a few days later. The kids and I were staying at Wendy and Arnie's for the weekend. In anticipation of the potentially *very* long-distance phone call, I carefully laid out pen and paper on the bed in the guest room. I didn't have a tape recorder handy, but I did plan to copy down any words of advice that Michael, via Rebecca, might care to relay. I watched the clock with the anxiety of a teenager waiting to hear from a crush and placed the call at precisely the appointed time.

"Hello," I said, "this is Isabel Ackerman. You know . . . Ivana's friend?"

"Oh hi, Isabel," she said, sounding a bit disconcerted. I tried to overlook the slight ditziness in her voice. This was a woman who spoke to dead people. Who wouldn't sound a little spacey?

"Look, Isabel, I'm sorry, but my daughter got sick and I had to take her to the doctor. It's put me a little behind. Can we reschedule for next week?"

Reschedule??!! I wanted to scream at her, I can't reschedule! I've been waiting to talk to my dead husband for a week now! In all the years I've known him we've never gone this long without talking to each other! I want to know what he has to say for himself! I want to know what I should do! HOW CAN I POSSIBLY RESCHEDULE???!!!

Instead I said casually, "Yeah, sure. No problem. What would be a convenient date and time?"

A few minutes later I slunk down the stairs to the kitchen. Wendy and Arnie were picking at the remains of lunch and looked at me with anticipation.

"Well?" Wendy asked anxiously. "What did she say?"

"She said that her daughter got sick and that she had to reschedule for next week."

"Ha!" Arnie shot back skeptically, his mouth full of what looked to be cole slaw. He was a nice guy, a good father, and a faithful husband whose belief system was firmly grounded in the conviction that the Mets were a better team than the Yankees. "Not much of a psychic, is she?" he crowed. "You'd think she'd have known her daughter would get sick *before* she scheduled the appointment."

"But *she* didn't schedule the appointment, smarty pants," I told him, the smell of pickles in the air. "Her assistant did. So there!"

But privately I had my doubts.

Nevertheless, three days later found me beside the phone, sitting in my living room, pen and paper again at the ready.

"I'm so sorry about your loss, Isabel."

Her voice was thin and reedy, like a capricious little girl's.

"Thanks."

"Michael said that you shouldn't worry. Everything will be OK."

Maybe Arnie was right. She did sound a little lame.

"I see a wood floor," she went on. "All around there's wood."

Funny. With the carpet out being cleaned, that's all I saw, too.

She went on gently. "It wasn't his heart, you know. It was his head. He had a bad headache, blinding, and then everything just . . . stopped."

I felt the tears starting.

"He's not in pain anymore, Isabel. And he's with someone named Ruth. Do you know who that is?"

I took a sharp breath and shifted my position on the couch. "His mom. Her name was Paula. Paula Ruth." A week before Michael's sixteenth birthday she had kissed him good night and gone to bed. When he woke up the next morning, she was being carried out by paramedics. Her death and his grief and sense of responsibility had become an essential part of his core. You could smell it on his skin like aftershave.

Rebecca paused for a moment and then went on.

"He's trying to show me something. It looks like . . . it looks like the Book of Solomon."

Michael's supposed middle name. I couldn't help but laugh.

"He says he feels bad, Isabel. Feels bad about leaving you with the girls . . . all that responsibility, and so close to your wedding anniversary. September seventeenth, isn't it?"

Holy God! How did she know that?

"He says he has faith in you, though. That you'll come through." Easy for him to say, I thought, grabbing a pillow for ballast. "He's also saying something about the number twenty-five. Does that mean anything to you?"

"Well," I said, wracking my brain, "I was around that age when I moved to New York."

I tried to take this all in. I wanted to believe her. Believe that Rebecca was sitting in her sunny West Coast kitchen conversing with Michael as if he had just dropped in for a cup of coffee. It was true she knew about many things . . . Michael's mother's name, our anniversary. But I was waiting. Waiting for her to tell me something so I would know for sure and without a doubt that this wasn't all some kind of con.

"Is that all?"

"Pretty much. He says again that he loves you and the girls."

I rolled my tear-stained eyes: a drop bounced off the sheet of paper. Then Rebecca spoke again.

"Wait a second. Michael says to tell you 'It's supposed to tickle.' "

"What!?"

"Oh," said Rebecca, presumably to Michael, "I understand."

To me she said, "Michael says behind your left ear. When he kisses you there. He says, 'It's supposed to tickle.' "

And with that, for sure, I knew.

After reluctantly hanging up with Rebecca—Are you sure there's nothing else, I wanted to ask? Does he have any solid words of advice?—I immediately picked up the phone and called Wendy.

"Do you believe it was Michael?" she asked.

"I do."

"Then I do, too."

She was just about to hang up when Arnie came on the line.

"She must have read the obit in the newspaper," he said.

"She lives in Southern California!"

"Maybe she gets *The New York Times.*"

"It wasn't in *The New York Times.* And besides, we live in New Jersey. If it was anywhere it would have been in the *Star-Ledger.* And no one gets the *Star-Ledger* if they don't live in New Jersey. Trust me, it's not that exciting."

"Maybe she picked it up on the Internet," suggested Arnie.

"Oh come on," I said, as the absurdity of defending a psychic who spoke to dead people suddenly dawned on me. I plowed on anyway. "Even if she did know that Michael died, how would she know about my left ear?"

As a last resort, my brother-in-law suggested *I* must have inadvertently told Rebecca during our phone conversation and she made it sound as though *she* was telling me.

"I may be in mourning, but I'm quite sure I'm not *that* much of an idiot," I told him with a laugh.

"Hey," Arnie asked, "did Michael have a message for me?"

"As a matter of fact, Arnie, he did."

"Really?"

"Yeah. He said that maybe you should be a Yankee fan. They win more often."

There was silence on the other end of the line, and for a second I thought he had hung up.

"You know what?" Arnie said. "It comes to me suddenly that having faith in the Mets is kind of like believing in psychics. It goes against popular opinion but deep down it just feels right. So I'm thinking, Isabel, maybe that lady in LA did speak to Michael. And I want you to ask her to tell Michael that I'm gonna stick with the Mets. And that he shouldn't worry. Your sister and I will be looking after you, too."

A few days later the medical examiner called to tell me that Michael had died of a brain hemorrhage. "It happened very suddenly," she told me, her words echoing Rebecca's. "He had a bad headache. And then everything just . . . stopped."

The psychic's message from Michael had been reassuring in an abstract kind of way, but it did nothing on a visceral level, where the doors were blown off and the wind scorched through. Life was moving on even if I wasn't ready to move with it. I spoke to clients. I sent out press releases. I made phone calls. I opened my mail. The flood of sympathy cards—from friends, family, friends of friends, friends of family—was overwhelming. I wondered if Hallmark had noticed a spike.

A few days later, Ivana took Austin, along with Jenna and Sadie, to the park for a couple of hours to give me some time to catch up. At three, I gave up the pretense of getting anything done and headed downstairs to meet the kids. I was a few minutes early, and I wandered out back, past the well-manicured lawn and summer flowers, down to the path that led to the lower parking lot.

The day after Michael died, Ivana moved his car from the parking lot out front to the lower lot by the back door. She felt it would be easier for the kids and me not to see the car every time we left the building, and she was right. But here we were face-to-face, my skin hot and wet with tears and Michael's Subaru, sad and abandoned, Jenna's school picture strung up with pink yarn dangling from the rearview.

I sobbed. I swore. I cursed. I climbed through the Subaru's hatchback and wrapped my arms around Michael's gym bag as if it were a child. I could have stayed inside forever—sweating and crying—but the temperature inside the car hovered around ninety-seven degrees and I felt as if I might pass out. So I uncurled myself and climbed out from the back, eyes blurring in the sun, when something lying next to Michael's right front tire caught my attention. It looked like a discarded pen cap. Curious—and it's hard to be curious and sob at the same time—I bent down to take a closer look. It was a feather, about three inches long, in a thousand shades of blue. I picked it up and walked back toward the front entrance where Ivana would be arriving with Austin, Jenna, and Sadie.

She pulled up just as I reached the front door, feather still clutched in my hand. She looked at me and then at the feather.

"My grandmother used to say that feathers are messages sent from heaven."

Did she indeed.

Time continued to move forward as time is wont to do. I came to a point that winter where I accepted that Michael was watching over us. "Our" song, an old cover of "Groovy Kind of Love" crooned by Phil Collins, played on the radio almost constantly. Endless Elvis movies—Michael's favorite—appeared on television with sudden regularity. And feathers began appearing in the most unusual places. I finally told Michael point-blank that he better not appear before my eyes because my heart certainly couldn't take it.

But here's the thing. The instant I accepted it, I realized that it didn't matter whether Michael was looking over us or not. He was still not in my bed at night or there when the kids woke up in the morning. Unless he was planning to come back in the body of Whoopi Goldberg as Patrick Swayze had in *Ghost*, his unseen presence was more a reminder of what we had lost than of what still might remain.

We floated through the remainder of the year like the zombies my kids watched on *Scooby-Doo*. Jenna, now in third grade and wanting to fit in with her two-parent friends, refused to mention Michael's death.

"Did you tell Shannon?" I asked. I had just picked her up from school, and I glanced surreptitiously in the mirror to gauge her response.

"Tell her what?" she asked, immediately on guard.

"About Daddy."

"No," she answered coolly, staring implacably ahead.

"But why? She's been your best friend since kindergarten."

"I dunno," she responded. "It never came up."

Sadie, in her last year of preschool, was more likely to talk about her recent fall from the monkey bars than she was about the death of her dad.

In high school my nickname was Turtle, which was incongruous because I spent most of my late teens and early twenties moving quickly, eyes tightly shut, through life's numerous rough spots. My philosophy: If you couldn't see your problems, then you didn't have to deal with them. It took Michael's more gradual pace to finally slow me down.

Michael didn't make me whole by "completing me"; he made me whole by believing in me. His love and faith enabled me to begin the work of completing myself.

And then he was gone. And I couldn't seem to find my balance. So I incorporated the skills I had learned years before while jumping rocks at the neighborhood creek with my grandfather.

"The faster you move, the less likely you are to fall," he had told me.

My kids and I moved around so that I could avoid moving forward. There wasn't one weekend that first year that we were at home. When we weren't in Long Island visiting Michael's family, we were in Philadelphia visiting mine. My form of escape was to simply try to outrun the pain.

Pity I had such short legs.

When we did slow down, it was to a life I couldn't get a handle on. Work—pitching stories about underwear and the newest Chia Pet—was alternately crazy busy and deadly slow. The kids were either deeply disconsolate or tentatively happy. It was like living on the edge of a surfboard, one day at the top of a wave and the next in the shallows. The one constant was our bedtime routine. At 9:00 P.M. I double-locked the front door, turned off the lights, and crawled into bed with my kids.

I was not anxious to sleep alone. Acres of white sheets, once warm and welcoming, now unfurled across my bed like polar ice caps along the tundra. It was true that, with no one but myself to consider, I could stay up late watching TV and gorging on Häagen-Dazs. And if that wasn't reason enough to rejoice, I could now crawl into the center of my big empty bed and enjoy the extra room. But to me it seemed more lonely than secluded—desolate, empty, and cold.

Even on the warmest nights, when the heat came up in hot blasts, I slept with my arms around my girls, trying to get as close as I could to the memory of Michael there beside me. We talked about the day, cried about our fate, and pretended to grab ice-cream cones from out of the sky.

"I want blueberry!" Sadie shouted, one tiny hand wrapped around my hair while the other reached toward the ceiling.

"I want chocolate, chocolate chip," I said next, trying to keep my spirits up and my eyes open. "With a cherry!"

"I want Daddy," said Jenna, tears welling in her eyes. She had immediately taken possession of Michael's pillow after he died and covered it with one of his old striped T-shirts. It traveled with her, in a bag with her stuffed dog Mystic, everywhere she went.

"It's not fair," she wailed, clutching the pillow.

My heart pounded in my chest. The grief I had for my loss was nothing compared to the grief I felt for my girls.

Six months after the food was gone and the sympathy cards had ceased, Phoebe continued to check in by phone every day.

"How you doing?" she asked one snowy afternoon in January.

"OK," I responded. "How *YOU* doing?"

"Not so good."

I sat down on the sofa.

"Tell me."

"I can't tell you. You've got enough problems."

"Me and the rest of the world. Tell me what's the matter."

"I don't want to burden you."

"Phoebe . . . I swear to God if you don't tell me what's wrong I'm gonna come up there and steal all your Jimmy Choos."

"Who cares? You know that when I die I'm gonna leave them to you anyway."

"Phoebe!"

"All right," she signed. "It turns out that Henry's been filling more than just cavities."

This was news I hadn't expected. I stood and began to absently pace.

"You sure?"

"Of course I'm sure. The idiot admitted it!"

She stifled what sounded like a sob.

"The tall, brunette dental hygienist?"

"No. The short, blonde part-time receptionist." She put down the phone to blow her nose. "It's funny," she said a few moments later. "Seems like it was only yesterday that *I* was the girl men left their wives for. Getting old . . . ain't it a bitch?"

"Yeah, just like Henry's part-time receptionist."

"It's not her fault," Phoebe said. I was surprised how quickly she sprang to the woman's defense.

"It's not?"

"No. It's not. It's Henry's. And it's even a little mine. You were with Michael for twelve years and never knew his middle name or that he wasn't half Irish. And I was with Henry for almost that long and never knew he was a cheating, low-down dirty slut."

"I think that's a different thing, Phoeb."

"No, it isn't. It's *exactly* the same thing. You think you know a person . . . you build a life with them, you want to have their kids . . . you even have sex with them when you don't feel like it. Just to find out later that they're not Irish, their middle name isn't Solomon, and they can't keep their sorry little dicks in their pants!"

"I'm so sorry, Phoeb. Really I am. Are you going to ask him for a divorce?"

"I'd rather knock out all his teeth and replace them without Novocain but, yeah, I think I may have to settle for a divorce."

"Jeez, Phoeb."

"Some happy enchiladas we turned out to be, huh? So tell me, how are *you* doing?"

"You know how it is," I told her, reciting the rest of our song, the one that played on my stereo what seemed like a hundred years ago: 'You're up one day and the next you're down . . .' "

Phoebe joined me for the finish: "It's a happy enchilada and you think you're gonna drown, that's the way that the world goes 'round!"

CHAPTER NINE

I read somewhere that one needs silence in which to grieve. I ran from that silence as if it were the plague, certain that its effects would surely kill me.

But thanks to a noisy neighbor, I found that there was one sound I could live without—the one that rumbled through my ceiling and emanated from a saxophone. When it continued to blare incessantly from the apartment above mine, I took my complaints to Bob, my affable super.

"Must be Charlie Gordon," he said.

"Who's Charlie Gordon?"

"Your upstairs neighbor."

"I thought my upstairs neighbor was an eighty-year-old widow named Peggy."

"Nope. Peggy moved to an assisted living community last

month." Bob leaned toward me and chucked. "Couldn't hold her chardonnay. Now it's a divorced computer programmer who plays the sax."

"Well," I said, pulling myself up to my full height of five-feet nothing. "He needs to stop."

"OK," said Bob. "You tell him."

He gave me Charlie's phone number, and I immediately put in a call. I got an answering machine with a pleasant enough message and tried to speak civilly.

"This is your downstairs neighbor. Can it with the sax."

Perhaps understandably, I never got a call back. And the band played on.

The second time I called was in mid-concert. I could hear his phone ringing through my ceiling as it accompanied his sax. Again the machine picked up: "I'm not here right now. Please leave a message." Beep!

I was in the middle of a conference call with a big client from California when Charlie next fired up his horn.

"Hey, Isabel," said the big client, unaware that I worked out of my suburban apartment. "What's going on there? Sounds like you're in a strip club!"

By the time I hung up the phone thirty minutes later, I was ready to take Charlie out. Horizontally. I ran the stairs two at a time. Despite the fact that I pictured him like the majority of my neighbors as possibly old and most likely infirm, I planned to kick his butt.

I knocked. And then I banged. And finally Charlie opened the door. Smiling.

"Hey," he said in a voice I knew from his answering machine. "Can I help you?"

"I'm your downstairs neighbor."

He held out his hand. I let it hang there for a moment before taking it.

"I'm Charlie."

"I know. I've left you a couple of messages."

"Messages?"

"Yeah. Messages. You know those little things that you leave on the phone when someone calls and you're not home?"

Either he chose to ignore my sarcasm, or he was unaccountably slow.

"I'm sorry," he said, a trace of disdain in his voice. "I'm not that fond of the phone. I changed my service recently and . . ."

Charlie continued to talk. It was right about then that I stopped listening and began to observe. The first thing I noticed was that he was under the co-op's unofficial median age of eighty-five. He appeared to be in his mid-forties; stood about 5'8", and had a strong build and curly salt and pepper hair.

"Where are my manners?" he asked, slightly bowing in a gesture that must have seemed like a good idea at the time. "Would you like to come in?"

I stepped inside and looked around.

"I thought Bob said that you've been here about a month."

"About that."

Could have fooled me. There was hardly any furniture. The couch, slipcovered in worn green silk tapestry, was piled high with blankets and a pillow. In place of such niceties as coffee tables and picture frames were piles of magazines, stacks of record albums, and a sizable telescope. There was a television tuned to CNN and an old turntable to accommodate the records. The bookshelves were crammed with "light" fare by William S. Burroughs and Henry Miller and looked as if they were in danger of toppling over onto the floor, which was covered here and there with faded area rugs.

Despite the chaos, the space exuded warmth and was scented with a mix of clean laundry, old magazines, and limes, which, I would find out later, Charlie used to garnish his Belvedere martinis.

"Sorry about the mess," he said, waving his hand in the general direction of the living room.

"No, no," I responded. "It looks fine."

"So anyway, what'd you call about?"

"Well . . ." I said, regaining some of my earlier animosity, "I work from home and all the noise is really driving me crazy."

"Noise?" he asked with a pained expression. I felt immediately guilty. He responded by becoming overly repentant.

"You see I just got divorced a few months ago. I was in business with my ex—not something I'd recommend by the way—so I'm not only single but I'm also out of a job."

"Well, of course, we all have problems but—"

"I used to play jazz sax professionally. Saw some of the greats. Art Blakey, Miles, Coltrane." I actually detected a faraway look in his hazel eyes. "It was hip."

"Hip?"

"Yeah," he said with a smile. "Hip."

"So why'd you stop?"

"We had a baby on the way. Figured a master's degree in computer programming would make for a more stable career path. So I went to night school and got one."

He gestured vaguely in the direction of his degree, which was displayed proudly on his wall next to a child's drawing of an Eskimo.

"You went to night school to get a drawing of an Eskimo?"

"It's a self-portrait," he said stiffly, hands jammed in his pants pocket. "My daughter drew it."

"It's lovely," I lied.

"After not being able to find a computer gig, I figured I might be able to make some money playing my horn. Hence," he added with a smile that made his eyes crinkle at the corners, "the 'noise.' "

I smiled apologetically. Then something suspended from the makeshift desk in the corner caught my eye. It looked, at first, like dangling pen caps, though upon closer inspection I found it to be an Indian dream catcher. And hanging from it were several feathers in a thousand shades of blue.

"Something wrong?" Charlie asked.

"Nope, just looking around." But the feathers had taken me by surprise. How many men, besides, possibly, one of the Village People, had feathers hanging in their living rooms? Was it a sign? I had repeatedly asked Michael to send me someone to talk to. Was Charlie his response? Or was it all just a stupid coincidence?

"Well, look," I stammered. "I'm sorry things have been so tough for you. But I have to make a living, too, and I can't do it with that . . . music, uh, distracting me."

Charlie walked into the kitchen.

"Can I get you a glass of water? Vodka?"

"Vodka? Do I look like I need a vodka?" I asked, somewhat afraid that I might. "It's not even three o'clock yet."

Charlie's right eyebrow shot up sardonically, and he smiled. "In my experience it never hurts to ask. So . . . what about that glass of water?" I shook my head *no thanks,* and he filled a glass for himself from the tap. I followed him back into the living room and watched as he walked over to his record albums, which were casually leaning against the wall.

"Ever hear of Charlie Mingus? How about Chet Baker?" Before I could respond, he had pulled out an album and placed it on the turntable. He shut his eyes, attention focused on the music spilling from the giant speakers, providing me with a good opportunity to take another look at him. His otherwise handsome face still bore the scars of teenage acne. His mouth, in contradiction to the roughness of his skin, looked soft and vulnerable, making him seem both a trifle rough and terribly insecure.

I listened politely to the music for a few more minutes before making my move to leave.

"Listen, I'd like to stay but I really have to get back to work." It wasn't until I said it that I realized the "I'd like to stay" part was actually true.

Before I left, Charlie Gordon and I made a deal. We would talk at the start of each week to create a schedule. I would try not to plan phone time when he was playing. And he would try to practice when I was not around.

Our deal, when we made it, seemed to cover all the bases. But inevitably, our once-a-week "scheduling" calls grew into several conversations a day. Charlie's opening line was "Talk to me," and after so many months of deafening silence, I did. His sign-off was "I'm here," and for a woman who had recently lost the most important man in her life, this was assurance I desperately needed to hear.

After three weeks of phone calls, Charlie and I made plans to have dinner. It had been a particularly cold winter so far, and the forecast called for heavy snow. I left the girls with Ivana and met Charlie in the lobby. We took my car, our breath hanging in the air like so many icicles. The cavernous restaurant, due either to the quality of the food or to the weather, was empty, which seemed to please him.

"So," I said after ordering a glass of merlot. "To our first date?" Not even a year had passed since Michael died and nothing even remotely romantic had come up with Charlie, so I was basically fishing, afraid to ask a direct question for fear of getting an equally direct answer.

"How about 'To friends'?" Charlie replied.

"Friends?"

"Come on, Izzy. I'm coming off a bad divorce and you've been through some heavy shit."

"So?"

"So you shouldn't be rushing to start a new relationship. You need some time to get your equilibrium back." He paused, leaning back in his chair. "Trust me . . . I know about this kind of thing."

Charlie was right, of course. Life without my husband was a tough adjustment that, despite my forced optimism, came and went like Sadie's baby teeth.

"Besides," he added, "you and I are just too different for a serious relationship. If there's anything I learned from my last marriage, it's how important it is to have stuff in common."

"Last marriage?" I sat up straight. "How many have you had, exactly?"

"Two."

My initial inclination was to argue with him about the importance of "stuff in common," but after two marriages perhaps he did know better.

We spent the rest of the evening talking about our kids, our romantic histories, and what to order for dessert. By the time we finished sharing a crème brûlée, it had begun to snow, the white flakes making everything white and clean and quiet.

As if the world was starting all over again.

I saw no reason to share the anniversary of Michael's death with the kids, as they lived with the loss every day. So I ticked off the changes alone, sitting on the floor of my living room on a late August afternoon, on the same spot where I had found my husband three hundred sixty-five days before.

I was a young widow and a single mom—labels that, like "socialite" and "prostitute," required a certain skill set to carry off. I had learned how to steel myself in the company of married friends. I anticipated the empathetic looks and deeply felt condolences, comforting myself that I, too, was once part of a happy couple. I put one foot in front of the other and hoped that the floor wouldn't crumble beneath me.

But I was learning to look on the bright side, too. My business was booming, and I had enough work to hire two people, a first.

"Life is just *amazing*," said Ivana later, over tea and chocolate cookies. "When one door closes, somewhere else a window opens."

"Not in my apartment. In my apartment the windows stick."

Ivana frowned. "That's not what I meant."

"I know what you meant. But I'd prefer to be poor and still have Michael."

"Of course you would. But that's . . . how you say . . . the catch? No one ever said that you'd get to choose."

Not getting to choose encouraged me to look at what had come in through the open window.

Sadie was happy and injury-free, buzzing around like a deranged bee. Jenna was doing well at school and slowly losing the glazed look she'd had in her eyes since that terrible day last August. And even though we were technically "manless," the girls and I were hardly lacking in male company. My stepson David taught Sadie how to ride a two-wheeler; my uncle taught her to swim. Arnie was on hand to yank loose teeth; my older stepson Jordan took Jenna and Sadie on jaunts into the city. And my father taught them how to drive. When I tried to protest, he called me a hypocrite. He had sat me on his lap in a red Mustang convertible when I was just five.

And then there was Charlie. In the six months since we had met, our repertoire had grown from thrice daily phone calls to Tuesday night dinner at his place while the kids played with Austin at Ivana's. Charlie's apartment had changed from the home of an irritating neighbor to my alternative universe—a place without children to comfort, without bills to pay, without laundry to wash. A place where I discovered Chet Baker's music, Noam Chomsky's politics, the Linux operating system, and—slowly—myself, unmoored and alone without Michael.

"How are the kids doing?" Charlie asked, washing down a

pepperoni slice with a sip from his Belvedere martini. He had yet to purchase a dining-room table, so dinner often involved delivery pizza and salad, consumed while sitting cross-legged on the floor.

"Sadie seems fine, but Jenna still wakes up most nights crying for her dad."

"She's lucky she had such a good one, even if it was for a short time. My father was the great emasculator. He'd cut you down to size and leave the bloody pieces on the floor for my mother to clean up." He paused. "But then again, he was the one who introduced me to jazz. Ironic, huh? The person who inflicts the most pain is also the one who introduces you to your savior. Good lesson, though. Taking the good with the bad."

I nodded as he continued.

"Unfortunately it wasn't a lesson my older brother picked up. Kevin opted out at sixteen. Hung himself from a beam in his bedroom. My dad had kicked me out of the house by then—said I'd be lucky to end up a garbage man—so Kevin and I hadn't spoken in a while. I'll never forget when my mom called to tell me. I just felt numb. Cold and numb."

If nothing else, we certainly had that in common.

Phoebe, having filed for divorce, was also stumbling down the road of self-discovery.

"We put the house up for sale," she told me by telephone.

"Makes sense. Are you going to look for something else up there?"

"Nah. Westchester was Henry's choice. I never really liked it all that much. Too white bread."

"Too white teeth!"

Phoebe laughed. "That, too."

"So where?"

"I was thinking . . . and don't you dare laugh . . . of looking for a smaller place near my brother."

"The one who lives in New Jersey?"

"Yes," she sighed. "The one who lives in New Jersey."

"But that's great Phoebs! You'll be local again!"

"Yeah. Just like the tomatoes. So, how are things going with that upstairs neighbor of yours? You know . . . the trumpet player?"

"It's a sax, Phoebe."

"Same difference."

"Well, I might have considered a relationship, but he's decided to take the high road."

"Don't be silly, Isabel. Dating is like politics. There *is* no high road."

"Well, *he* thinks there is. He went through a bad divorce . . . I lost a husband. He thinks we should wait."

"Wait for what? It's over a year since Michael died." Phoebe sighed. "But maybe it's just as well. I seem to remember you saying that he wasn't cute and he didn't have a job."

"No. I said that *you* wouldn't think he was cute. But you're right about the second thing. He doesn't have a job."

"Still? Does he have any money?"

"Ivana thinks he's really an eccentric millionaire."

"What does he drive?" Phoebe asked. Henry the dentist drove a Porsche.

"A Jetta."

"A Volkswagen?"

"Last time I looked."

"He's not eccentric, Isabel. He's just poor. Why does Ivana think he's got money?"

"He always pays for dinner when we order in."

"He pays because he's a nice Jewish boy. And he orders in because he's probably wanted by the police. Has he met the kids yet?"

He had.

I introduced him to Jenna and Sadie simply as our upstairs neighbor. There was no pressure, no implied sense that he could be taking Daddy's place next to Mommy in the family Subaru. But unlike *my* first meeting with Charlie, there was no spark, no connection. To the contrary, they all behaved like strangers from a hostile planet.

But having never been a quitter, I tried to make it work. We hauled his eight-year-old daughter, she of the Eskimo self-portrait, to weekend activities like ice skating and pottery painting. She and Sadie hit it off—there's nothing like a bit of dress-up to break the ice—but Jenna never got into the spirit of things. After one particularly strenuous meal at Friendly's when we waited for two hours because the waitress forgot to put in our order, Jenna inquired as to whether we would all live together if Charlie and I got married.

"Well . . . it's really not that kind of relationship," I tried to explain to her.

"What do you mean?"

"I mean it's not the marrying kind of relationship."

"Then what kind of relationship is it?" Jenna asked, echoing Phoebe's query.

How could I explain to my daughter and my best friend that it was the kind of relationship that, when the world was cold and dark, provided a safe place to hide? It was a *folie à deux*. And nothing less would have saved me.

Chanukah was approaching. And because Santa regularly stopped at our house, Christmas was coming, too. Brightly wrapped piles of gifts cluttered our already cluttered apartment, while bulging cartons of ornaments, multicolored candles, and a stately silver menorah—all pulled out from storage—balanced precariously on top of the piles.

Michael had always had a tree when he was growing up—it was the one tradition his mom couldn't bear to renounce when she cut her southern gentile roots to become a New York Jew. My family was stricter. I was not allowed a tree—not even so much as a Chanukah bush. Although neither of them were especially religious, my parents drew the line at a visit to Santa and a drive through the non-Jewish neighborhoods to gaze at blinking colored lights and papier-mâché replicas of the baby Jesus.

All grown up, I decided to take the southern gentile route. Every year, a week or so before Christmas, Michael, the girls, and I would bundle ourselves up and drag home a tree from the lot by the local shopping center. Every year Michael would mutter, "This time we're getting a *small* tree," and every year we'd arrive home with a sticky, fragrant pine that scraped the top of our ten-foot ceiling. After placing the tree in the stand, where it always seemed to list to one side, the kids and I would unwrap and hang the ornaments while Bing Crosby crooned in the background and Michael picked pine needles off the carpet.

This multicultural free-for-all had been our tradition for

seven years, and despite the fact that I was now responsible for all the shopping, wrapping, packing, hauling, and driving, I was adamant that our ritual was not going to change. Of course it helped that my stepson David showed up dragging a tree that would have made Rockefeller Center proud.

"Usually when people come to visit they just bring a cake or something," I said as he propped the evergreen against the wall.

The girls ran out of their bedroom and straight into David's arms. Unlike his older brother Jordan, Michael's younger son was following a trajectory more in line with his father's. He dropped out of college in his second year and became a union carpenter. He was a first responder when the Twin Towers came down, and he took work—and life—as he found them.

"Where'd you find such a huge tree?" asked Sadie, dwarfed by the size of it.

"Well, I'll tell you," he said, hugging one half sister and then the other. "I was on my way home, minding my own business, when it just kind of jumped out at me and said, 'Bring me home to Jenna and Sadie.' "

David and I dusted off the tree stand and unpacked the ornaments. We took turns hanging the tinsel, one strand at a time. Then David lifted Sadie onto his shoulders so she could put the star at the top.

"Thank you for this," I told him after the kids, exhausted from excitement, were finally near sleep.

He brushed off the gratitude like snow on his Chevy pickup. "We're family, Isabel. With or without Dad. I'll be here whenever you need me."

I was tucking the kids into bed a few nights later when Sadie announced that she knew what she wanted for this year's Chanukah present. "Great," I said, expecting a request for yet another computer game, stuffed animal, or Barbie doll. I sat gingerly on her bed, trying to avoid squashing the multitude of stuffed animals that surrounded her.

"What is it you want, honey?"

"It's hard to explain," she replied, somewhat shyly.

"Was it something you saw on TV? In a catalog?"

Leaning on a little elbow, she screwed up her courage, and plowed straight ahead. "I want a daddy," she said. "I know you said we shouldn't care what the other kids have, but I'm the *only* one in my class who doesn't have one!"

"Well, that's kind of a tough request," I said, smoothing her hair.

She pulled away, having none of it.

"But why?"

"Because I can't run down to Toys 'R' Us to buy you one."

"Is it a money thing?"

"No. It's not a money thing."

"So what, then?" Sadie asked, her tiny arms now wrapped around her stuffed dog Daisy.

"Well . . . something like finding a daddy is going to require a bit of looking."

"Do you think you can find one in time for Chanukah? It comes later this year."

"Not that late, honey."

"Then what about for Christmas?" The look on my face must have been less than encouraging. "New Year's?"

I shook my head, kissed her good night, and told her I'd see what I could do.

"You're ready to date again so soon?" The lady taxi driver, who had been a widow at forty-five, turned and looked at me with a gimlet eye.

"Well . . ." I stuttered, "I *am* kind of lonely." When she clucked her tongue, I added in the bit about Sadie wanting a daddy. "How long did *you* wait?" I asked.

"Me? I haven't had so much as a cup of coffee with another man since my sainted husband passed twenty-two years ago."

The reproach hung in the stale taxi air like the pine-scented Christmas tree strung up from her rearview mirror. *Was* it too soon? Aside from what the man had advised at Michael's shivah— a scant thirty days of crying your eyes out—I had nothing else to go on. How long did Jackie Kennedy wait until she started seeing Ari? Priscilla after Elvis? Yoko after John?

I thought of Austin, Ivana's by now nine-year-old son, who in answer to the question of why he wanted a girlfriend replied, "Hey, I have *needs.*"

"Of course it's time to move on with your life!" proclaimed Jordan.

His father's sudden death had been hard on him, but Jordan's strategy for coping bore a striking similarity to mine: run as far and as fast as you can. In the sixteen months since his father died,

Jordan had graduated from college, moved to New York City, and found a job in advertising.

"It's not like you're not getting any younger!" he added. And then came the clincher. "And I know that Dad would agree with me."

"About which part?" But I knew he was right.

Michael had told me repeatedly, and usually with some exasperation, that I would be the last woman in his life. If I died first, he would choose to remain chaste. He had been kissing girls, he said, since his older sister brought home friends so they could practice on him.

But I was only forty when Michael died. I had, I hoped, years of heartbreak and laughter and great sex ahead of me. And although I knew it would be possible, I was certainly hoping not to have to do it all on my own.

CHAPTER TEN

Every Sunday night, Michael and I used to watch *Sex and the City*. And every Sunday night after it was over, I would turn to him and say, "Thank God I don't have to date anymore." Now, in order for me to fill Sadie's request, it seemed that I did. I had never got anything in my life without working for it, so I was fully prepared to roll up my sleeves, shave my legs, and begin the hunt. But having spent the decade married and huddled away in the suburbs, I had no earthly idea where to begin.

"Put on some makeup and a pair of heels," Phoebe told me from her perch on the edge of my bed. Having ditched her philandering husband, Phoebe, like me, was once again single and full of advice. "And for God's sake cover the gray!"

"You're a beautiful woman, Isabel," Charlie said the following Tuesday when I explained Phoebe's plan. "But . . ."

"But what?"

"But as long as you're considering an update . . ."

"You mean a makeover . . ."

"Update . . . makeover . . . whatever. I think you should lose the bangs."

"The bangs?" I reached for my forehead protectively. "I've had the bangs since I was seventeen!"

"Exactly my point. It's time for a grown-up haircut." This from a man who looked as though he still wore hand-me-downs.

"Anything else?" I asked him.

"Well . . . I'd do . . . what are they called? . . . Highlights. Just brighten things up a bit."

"You're giving me style advice?"

Charlie shrugged his shoulders. We were sitting on his old, worn couch, listening, as always, to jazz. "Any reason why I shouldn't?"

"I'll give you a couple of reasons. You're wearing a faded green T-shirt, an old man's watch, and an ugly brown belt to hold up your jeans, which, incidentally, are two sizes too big."

"I told you," he said, patting his stomach, "I lost some weight after the divorce. And it wouldn't be fiscally responsible for me to spend money on clothes until I get a job."

"Maybe so. But you won't get a job if it looks like your pants are about to fall down."

"To the contrary," he said, smiling. "For some jobs that could be a plus."

I arched my well-covered eyebrows. "I wasn't aware that those were the types of jobs you were interviewing for."

"So," Charlie asked, standing up to go to the kitchen to

refresh his drink. "What's the motivation for all this makeover stuff?"

"I dunno. I thought I'd stick a foot back in the dating pool." I reached for my drink and took a sip.

"Really?" he asked from the kitchen. "What made you decide that?"

"It's been a year and a half since Michael died. And you've been a great friend but I feel like I'm ready for a little . . . you know. More."

"More, huh." He sat back down next to me on the couch. He paused for a moment, carefully choosing his words. "You know I dig you, Isabel . . ."

"So you've said."

Charlie put down his drink and took another tack. "Are you familiar with that Nietzsche theory?"

"Which one?"

"The one that says 'Whatever doesn't kill us makes us stronger'?"

"I've heard it, yes. Why?"

"I think that whatever doesn't kill us just eats us alive . . . bit by bit . . . until at the end, all we need is a dent in the car or . . ." He looked directly at me and continued: ". . . a lousy-ass guy to push us over the edge."

"So what? Are you saying you're a lousy-ass guy? Or are you just afraid I'll end up with one?"

He paused for a minute. Then, as if in answer to my question, he sat up, leaned over, and kissed me. He was hesitant at first, as if his lips were trying to find exactly the right place to settle on mine.

And then they did.

The kiss was passionate, needy, questioning. I breathed him in as if he were oxygen. He put his arms around me and pulled me to the floor, his hands touching my face, my breasts, my hips. I held on to him for dear life while the rolling Cuban rhythm of *Buena Vista Social Club* wafted in the air like perfume.

"So, you finally did the deed, huh?" Phoebe asked, amused. "I swore I wasn't going to say anything but, jeez, it's about time."

We were sitting at my dining-room table eating peanut butter and jelly sandwiches while Jenna and Sadie watched a Disney movie in the living room. Phoebe had moved back to New Jersey a few months before and had found an apartment an hour away from mine. Being able to commiserate in person was just like the old days, except, on the whole, the quality of the furniture and the food were somewhat better.

"You're just jealous."

"You bet your ass," answered Phoebe, reaching for her second half. "Was it good? And don't say he played you like a sax or I'll have to throw up."

"It was great. But I'm not sure what it means."

"It has to mean something?"

"Come on, Phoebe. It's not as if we haven't known each other for a while. And it happened right after I told him I was going to start dating again."

"Ah . . . sex as a delay tactic. I like it."

"Seriously."

"Seriously. I think you should keep your head up and forge ahead."

"Meaning?"

"Go join a gym."

"A gym? Are you kidding? Michael made me join every gym within twenty miles of the apartment."

"Do you go?"

"Of course not. But that doesn't stop Jack LaLanne from billing me every month."

"Izzy, you've been a couch potato since I met you. And you were married to a gym guy!"

"So?"

"Do you have any idea what the other gym guys must have been saying about you behind Michael's back?"

I was reaching for my second sandwich but thought better of it. "You're kidding me, right?"

"We're getting older, Isabel. Go to the gym. You'll live longer and feel better. Besides, who knows who might be working out on the next treadmill? The best way to meet a guy is just to get *out there.*"

"Out *where* exactly?" I stood up to glance into the living room and check on the kids. "You live in the suburbs. You know the drill. This is the land of the Junior League, PTA meetings, and family picnics. The only unmarried guys in Montclair march either with the Boy Scouts or in the Gay Pride parade. Trust me. I've checked. And what about you? The divorce is final, isn't it? Have you been getting *out there?*"

"Forget about me," Phoebe said, tossing the crust onto her plate. "I'm signing up to become a nun."

"No designer clothes."

"OK, so maybe I'll sign up to be a lesbian."

"So," I asked Charlie over the phone. I could still detect the smell of him on my skin from the night before. "What do we do now?"

"Now?"

Charlie often claimed his thirty years of therapy had made him open to "looking" at his "stuff," but a conversation about our relationship seemed as impossible to accomplish as Sadie's wish to fly.

"Yes. Now. Now that we've made love, had sex, done the groove thing."

"You know how I feel about you, Isabel, but it's just too soon."

"But we've known each other for over a year!"

"Still, I don't think either one of us is ready for a serious relationship. A commitment."

"But we're *already* in a relationship. I'm *already* committed."

But aside from our Tuesday night ritual—now expanded from dinner, drinks, and conversation to include some extremely passionate sex—he didn't seem to agree.

Phoebe's advice? "Forget about him."

But Charlie, I was finding, was not so easy to forget. His happy-go-lucky facade hid a well of despair that was as compelling to me as crack to an addict. If I concentrated on *his* pain—his unhappy marriages, his separation from his kids, his inability to find a job—I would focus less on mine. In a way I couldn't quite understand, we seemed to be each other's best hope.

The following Tuesday, I was cleaning up after our regular a dinner of salad and pizza while Charlie set up the chessboard. He was trying, so far with little success, to teach me how to play. The rain slamming against the old windows accompanied the music playing on the stereo. Charlie paused mid-setup and literally cocked his head.

"What's that sound?"

"Is this a test?" I sneaked a peak at the record currently on the turntable. "I think it's Charlie Mingus."

"Yes, it *is* Mingus and I saw you look at the album cover. But that's not what I meant."

I listened. "All I hear is the rain."

"Really? To me it sounds like singing. Like a choir of deranged angels . . . singing."

The apartment building's position high on a hill subjected it to tremendous gusts of wind. And the sound of the wind blowing through the building sounded exactly like deranged angels . . . singing.

"I don't have many friends, you know." Charlie said this softly, his hands jammed in his pockets, attention focused on the chessboard.

"As far as I can tell you don't have *any* friends."

He flashed a small smile. "Now that's just plain mean."

I reached over to touch his cheek. "Sorry."

"Where was I?" he asked.

"Not many friends . . ."

"Right. So I want you to know, Isabel," and here he took my hand, raised it to his lips, and kissed my palm, "how important our friendship is to me. And how beautiful I think you are."

I rolled my eyes.

"Seriously, baby. Inside and out. I don't know what I'd do without you."

I regained possession of my hand, looked at the board hopelessly, and moved a piece.

Charlie, in turn, took my bishop.

Had I done a little research, I might have recognized his behavior for what it was: a classic example of passive aggressiveness.

But I didn't. I was having too much fun. So I just kept playing the game.

I had found Charlie when I wasn't looking. How hard could it be to find a date when I was? I was a working publicist. A suburban mother. I had childhood friends, college pals, work acquaintances, and really nice neighbors. I knew a *lot* of people. I *told* a lot of people. Yet no one, NO ONE, offered to fix me up.

"I thought the 'fix-up' was like a tradition . . . part of our heritage, even."

Phoebe and I were having one of our regular phone chats.

"I don't know, Izzy . . . but a blind date?" Her voice went up an octave. "I remember blind dates. They can be bad. Real bad."

My mind flashed back thirty years to my mom's friend's son—a quiet guy with Coke-bottle glasses who excused himself to go to the bathroom and came back a few minutes later stark naked.

"And think of some of the ugly ones," Phoebe continued, *"twenty years later."*

I could hear her shiver through the telephone.

"We're older now," I said. "Perhaps we're not so shallow?"

"Oh, don't kid yourself, Izzy. Of *course* we're still that shallow! Maybe all those people you know . . . maybe they're not sure you're ready to date again."

Hardly. I had followed Phoebe and Charlie's advice: highlighted my hair, grew the bangs, wore clothes that actually fit, and forced myself to work out every morning after dropping the kids off at school. The gym was a place at once familiar and strange, where I imagined Michael's encouragement—"One more! Push it out!"—echoing over the grunts of my tattooed and sweaty companions. But what started as a possible way to meet cute boys soon turned into an all-consuming four-day-a-week routine. My endorphins rose to previously unseen levels, as did my once flaccid biceps.

"How could they not know I'm ready to date again? Frankly, there's no man, woman, or child I haven't told."

"Well maybe you have to tell them LOUDER," Phoebe shouted. "In heels!"

"You can't fill a full cup," said my mother a few weeks later. We were at Arnie's surprise fortieth birthday party, and I was munching on some hors d'oeuvres while scanning the living room for cute, single accountants.

"I'm sorry, Mom . . . but what the hell does that mean?"

"It means that you're not going to find someone as long as you're with someone else." She casually lifted a vase in my sister's living room to determine its provenance. "You're using Charlie as a safety net, Izzy. You won't be able to fly on your own as long as you've got one arm wrapped around him."

I was barely up to walking briskly, yet here she was worried that I wouldn't be able to fly.

But I knew that she was right.

It had been over a year and my relationship with Charlie had grown as stagnant as the putty-colored water in Sadie's fish tank. I wanted more. He couldn't, or wouldn't, give it. We continued with our once-a-week dinners and our daily phone calls. But every time he made a commitment to deviate from the regular Tuesday night schedule, it would usually result in an e-mail cancelation early the day of the date. Charlie continually drew me in with one hand and pushed me away with the other. I began to think that my upstairs neighbor was a spy or, perhaps, someone else's husband.

When I told him of my suspicions he laughed. "I wish I could tell you I had a double life. Truthfully, with the way this one is going, two might actually kill me."

Some days Charlie found it difficult to curb his frustration at his reduced circumstances, but those days were mostly few and far between. He ultimately believed he would find a great job, play the big clubs. I was usually his first call after he got the bad news, and it was painful to watch him get his hopes dashed on such a regular basis. When it came to his shortcomings, I realized, Charlie lived on the south side of denial. Not that I wasn't there most days keeping him company.

"Everything will be all right," I told him after one particularly bad interview, hoping that it would.

"You know," he said irritably, "sometimes you sound like you're reciting lines from a movie script."

"I suppose that comes from watching too many of them."
Next to Charlie, a Wednesday matinee was my greatest escape.

But a month later, when Charlie stood me up for Passover, I
knew I needed to broaden my horizons.

"Look, I think the Jews need to get over that whole out-of-
bondage thing. It sounds so Lower East Side."

"But you promised!" I said, hurt once again by his rejection
and his inability to commit.

"And they need to update the plagues. I mean, who gives a
shit about locusts nowadays? Roaches, bad subway service, AIDS,
and Republicans . . . now you're talking!"

"So how was Passover?" Phoebe asked over lunch in the city.

"Fine," I said between bites of salad. "We sang a few songs,
hid some matzo. The usual. Why? You thinking of converting?"

"No," she said, absently playing with her silverware. "Just
making conversation."

"Phoebe, we've been friends since before my boobs dropped.
Since when have you had to make conversation?"

She dropped her knife and bent to retrieve it, her voice floating up from the floor. "Since I wanted to figure out how to get you
to go on a blind date."

"I thought you said blind dates were bad!"

"Well," she said, sitting up again. "They are bad. But this one
isn't blind because I know him, so really it's just a little nearsighted."

"Why don't *you* go out with him?"

"I told you. I'm swearing off men for a while. Trust me, Iz.
John's a really nice guy. I know him from high school."

"When's the last time you saw him? And stop playing with the damn silverware!"

"The prom," she said, crossing her hands in front of her.

"The senior prom?"

"Yeah. I didn't go to the junior prom."

"Phoebe!"

"I'm kidding. I ran into him the other day in town and he looked pretty good. Divorced father of two. Or maybe it's three. Anyway, he owns his own business—something to do with construction, I think."

"Is he Jewish?"

"Since when do you care if he's Jewish?"

"Since that's the way it was with Michael, and I thought it would be easier than just starting over with a Mormon or something."

"Well, he's not a Mormon. But I don't think he's Jewish either. He does, however, live around the corner from me. Just think of it. If you two get married you can come down to Jericho to live!"

Jericho, New Jersey, was a place of scenic farmland whose vistas were broken only by acres of trailer parks and the occasional 7-Eleven. Although I loved Phoebe, unless John was George Clooney's cloned twin, I didn't plan on moving anywhere.

Despite this, and the fact that I hadn't been on a date since the year of the first AIDS breakout, I was game. I had fallen prey to the fairy tales—blind dates leading with insane briskness and great expediency to a big wedding and a blissful marriage. Love at first sight. Belonging. Destiny.

After all, how bad could he be? One had to begin somewhere, I reasoned, and it may as well be with John from Jericho. I spoke to him on the phone, a short conversation during which we set an agreeable time to meet. I put on mascara and blush, a vanity I had neglected with Charlie, and told the kids that I was meeting a friend for dinner.

"Who?" asked Sadie.

"Just a friend."

"What friend?" chimed in Jenna. "And how come your face looks so pink?"

"The trick," Phoebe explained, her voice booming out of my speakerphone, "is to look sexy but not like a s-l-u-t."

I could see Jenna's eight-year-old brain working. She had made the decision—without the encouragement of Phoebe or Charlie—to grow out her bangs, too. The new do added a sophistication that took my breath away.

"What's a 'lut'? she asked curiously. "And why don't you want to look like one?"

After another thirty minutes, I was as ready as I was ever going to be.

I met John downstairs in the lobby. He arrived on time in a jumbo-size SUV, wearing a plaid button-down shirt and jeans. He had closely cropped hair of an indistinguishable color and a thin frame and, while not horribly unattractive, there were no initial fireworks either.

"Where would you like to eat?"

He didn't know Montclair all that well, and we had agreed to play it by ear.

"There's a bunch of restaurants over on Church Street," I suggested. It was warm for early March, and Church Street was known for its quaint antique shops and local boutiques. It was a nice place to look around. Besides, I figured my nervousness wouldn't be as obvious if I kept on moving.

I was directing John out of my parking lot when he suddenly pulled the SUV over to the side of the road and stopped. Uh-oh, I thought. If he starts taking off his clothes, I am *so* outta here.

"Hey," he said. "Do most of the restaurants around here have liquor licenses or is it BYOB?"

After loosening my grip on the door handle, I told him that most places were bring your own. He pulled the SUV out onto the road again and asked if I minded if we stopped at a liquor store.

"No," I said. "Of course not."

I'd never been much of a drinker. All in all I'd rather have a mediocre black-and-white milk shake than a good glass of merlot. But a buzz isn't a bad thing, especially on a blind date. As we entered the nearby liquor store, I figured that Phoebe's high-school friend could manage to pick out something suitable without my help.

I milled around the store, admiring the pretty labels, until I heard my name from across the shop.

"Isabel! How's this?" John shouted, holding up what looked like a gallon of Stoli.

"It's vodka," I hollered back, thinking suddenly of Charlie and his Belvedere.

"Yeah, I know it's vodka. Great on ice."

Alrighty then.

He paid, and we hopped back into his SUV and lumbered on over to Church Street. After strolling around the block, brown bag clutched securely under his arm, we decided on Taro, which, the menu indicated, specialized in "eclectic Asian cuisine." The interior of the place was beautiful—all soaring bamboo, muted green walls, and dark wood. I half expected a cheetah to swing by with the menus.

Five minutes after we were seated John ordered two glasses with ice and a couple of appetizers.

"To a successful evening," he offered.

Not sure what a "successful evening" might entail but fairly sure this wouldn't be one, I raised my glass and followed his lead. He drained his shot before my first sip had worked itself halfway down my windpipe. Perhaps he was Russian. Either way, I was glad I wasn't driving back to Jericho with him.

So here I was. Single mom. In the rain forest. On a date. Apparently with an egomaniac. We talked about *his* divorce, *his* business, *his* kids. Every time I worked a foot into the conversation he managed to push it right out again.

"I like self-sufficient women, you know? My first wife was a JAP. I won't make that mistake again!"

I smiled. That certainly let me off the hook. I had a bathroom full of shoes and handbags . . . you couldn't get much JAPpier than that.

"And I like 'em slim. No fatties for me!" he said, draining his third glass and sucking on the lime.

Well, I thought—not that I cared—at least I measured up in that department.

"Yup. Slim. After my divorce, my ex gained thirty pounds."

After Michael died, I went in the opposite direction, losing fifteen pounds on what I called my finding-my-husband-dead-on-the-floor diet. I presently weighed 103 pounds and wore a size two. I was mulling this over as John continued.

"She used to be a skinny thing, but now she's . . . like you."

I swallowed a small piece of my pistachio-crusted jumbo shrimp. "Like me?"

"Yeah. I noticed when you got out of the car . . . kind of big from behind, aren't ya?"

"Big?"

Had I heard him wrong? Was it the vodka or the "eclectic Asian cuisine"? I needn't have worried because he repeated the comment.

Four more times.

So this is what modern dating was like. Sparkling conversation and insults.

"So what happened?" Phoebe asked.

I was lying in bed with the phone to my ear. Phoebe was the first person I called upon returning home from my first blind date since before the turn of the century.

"Let's just say that your original assessment of the blind date was right on target."

"That bad, huh?"

"He said I had a large posterior."

"A large posterior?"

"Uh-huh. But he didn't say it as nicely, and he said it in about seven different languages."

"You're kidding."

"Unfortunately, I'm not."

"Did you hit him with your cocktail?"

"Not quite. But I did have a second drink. Oh . . . and I ordered two desserts."

"Well," Phoebe said, "I tried. Sounds like John's too much of an ass for you."

"Yeah," I added, "and my ass is too much of an issue for John!"

CHAPTER ELEVEN

Spring had sprung, and the kids and I were having lunch with Jordan at a crowded trattoria in the city where I was drinking wine at noon. While filling him in about my doings in Montclair—school concerts and trips to the mall—Jordan enlightened me about dating in the twenty-first century.

"Finding a guy is easy," he said, taking a bite of his cheeseburger.

"Yeah . . . and if you're happy and you know it clap your hands."

"Isn't that what Barney sings?" asked Sadie, busy coloring on the paper tablecloth.

"How would you know?" asked Jenna. She looked back up at Jordan. "Mama doesn't let us watch Barney."

"It's crapola, right, Mommy?" said Sadie proudly.

"Yes, honey. It's crapola."

"You lost me," said Jordan. "Who's Barney? And what are we talking about again?"

"Dating. It's never been easy in *my* lifetime. I can't believe things have changed *all* that much."

"Of course they have! Don't you watch *Sex and the City*?"

"I'm one hundred years older than those girls, Jordan. I have two kids and I live in the suburbs. And I can't walk in—or afford—those shoes."

"Did you know," Jenna asked her brother, "that Mommy keeps her shoes in the bathtub?"

"Yes, honey, I know," he said, smiling at her. "Silly, isn't it?" Then, to me, "What about that neighbor you've been hanging out with?"

"Charlie? He's just a friend."

"A friend, huh? You sure you're not withholding?"

"OK . . . so maybe a little." I glanced at the kids. Jenna was sketching the flower arrangement perched at the hostess stand, and Sadie was drawing puppies.

I smiled and dropped my voice an octave. "Let's just say that he's a friend with *benefits.*"

"Really?" Jordan perked up. "Blue Cross *and* Blue Shield?"

I smiled.

"No wonder you're looking so good. So what's the problem?"

"He thinks he's got my number."

"Your cell phone number?" asked Jordan, confused.

"No. My *number* number. He thinks that even though I say I'm ready to commit it's really about my not wanting to be alone."

"Which is true," said Jordan, nodding.

"Which *may* be *partly* true," I conceded. "He thinks he's transition boy."

"For someone who hasn't had a job in a while he sounds like a smart guy."

"He *is* a smart guy," I said. "And he's interviewing."

"For what?"

"Depends on the day. Mondays and Wednesdays it's usually computer stuff. Fridays and Saturdays it's the sax."

"Sounds like a *busy* guy."

"That's what he says."

Jordan chewed on a french fry thoughtfully. "I know!" he said, practically leaping from his chair. "Have you checked out Match dot com?"

"Match dot what?"

He stared at me incredulously. "Oh my God! You've never heard of Match?"

"I was with your father for twelve years. All I know about modern dating is what I picked up on HBO. And it makes me scared, Jordy. Very scared."

"Match dot com is an Internet dating site. I met a great guy on Match a few weeks ago."

"Wow. You can find gay guys, too?"

"Yup. All kinds. And there's another one too . . . JDate."

"What's the difference?"

"JDate is for Jews."

"You're kidding me, right?"

"Nope. Not kidding. You put in where you live and what you're looking for and pictures of different guys pop up."

"Wow. It sounds kind of like eBay."

"Yeah. It *is* kind of like eBay. Tougher return policy, though."

We finished lunch and caught a movie. Then the girls and I drove back to Montclair. As soon as they were tucked into bed, I ran to my computer and grabbed my mouse. I went to Match.com first, and, true to Jordan's word, it was amazing. Pages and pages of men—tall, short, blond, sporty, bookish.

After searching the site for half an hour, I found an interesting-looking specimen whose screen name was Mad4u. Mad was handsome, his profile contained no spelling errors, and he said he loved kids. I was just about to find out what he was looking for in a woman when I was suddenly cut off.

"Come back!" I yelled at the screen, which promptly informed me that in order to continue "shopping" I needed to sign up for the service. I rifled through my wallet for my American Express card and punched in the numbers with lightning speed. Filling out the requisite background information took a bit longer.

Hmmm . . . Relationship status. "Widow with two kids" sounded too morose. "Divorced" didn't work. Perhaps I could say I was separated? It was, after all, technically true. Undecided, I left the space blank and moved on to physical description. Height and eye color were easy—five-feet nothing, newly highlighted golden brown hair, and large, expressive brown eyes. Despite John from Jericho's assessment, I listed my body type as thin. No visible tattoos. But I hesitated when it came to age. I didn't look forty-one—so what the hell, I would be thirty-eight.

Next came the more challenging part. I needed to write about who I was and what I was looking for in a match. *Well first off,* I typed, *I don't have a lot of baggage* (lie), *I have a cheerful disposition* (most of the time), *and I am totally happy with my life* (not quite true). *Also,* I wrote, *I'm totally honest* (except, I thought, when filling out dating profiles).

As simple as it sounded, all that was left to do was choose and download a picture. My grandfather had once accused me of purposely sabotaging family photos, as if I chose to look like a short, pre-electrolysis version of Cher on a very bad day. So I looked through inexhaustible stacks of dusty snapshots—Michael and me when we were dating, Michael and me after we got engaged, Michael and the kids—to find something that resembled my newly single, side-parted and highlighted, thirty-eight-year-old self.

I finally found a picture that didn't make me look like the Bride of Frankenstein, scanned it into my computer, and e-mailed it over to Match. Then I closed my tired eyes and envisioned my perfect man, sitting at his home computer in his nicely decorated living room, dressed in jeans and a smoking jacket, waiting for me to appear.

And then I waited. And waited.

Somehow I expected that I would be immediately barraged with messages. But I sat there, going back and forth from my in-box to my four hundredth page of matches. My eyes were growing blurry, until, at 1:27 A.M., I could no longer tell a loafer from a heel.

"You still sleeping with the sax player?" Phoebe asked. We were meeting for a quick lunch and a short run through Bergdorf's to look at all the new merchandise that I couldn't afford and that

Phoebe—who made six figures but was living in the land of the
discount mall—would never again pay retail for.

"You know," she said, checking out a pair of Jimmy Choo
sandals, "he's like that giant invisible squirrel James Dean hung out
with in that old movie."

"The movie was called *Harvey*, Phoebe," I said, gazing long-
ingly at a pair of Manolos. "With James *Stewart*. And it was a rabbit. Not a squirrel."

"Rabbit . . . squirrel. Who cares?"

"Well, I'm pretty sure the squirrel does."

"I'm your best friend, Izzy, and you've known this guy
how long?"

"Known him about a year and a half. Sleeping with him
about six months."

"OK. So tell me . . . if he's not just a figment of your imagi-
nation, why haven't I met him?"

"It's hard to explain, Phoebs. I'd say it's partly because I
know you don't approve and partly because he's just not husband
material."

The fact was, with Charlie still jobless and me now footing
the bill for most of our Tuesday night takeout, Charlie wasn't even
boyfriend material. But Charlie had, in some great measure, filled
some of the spaces left empty by Michael's sudden departure, and
his now-you-see-him-now-you-don't routine continued to keep me
distracted from the loss.

"So let me get this straight," Phoebe said. "He's got no
money and very little curb appeal. But it's been a year and a half so
he must be good for something."

"Well . . ."

"And I don't mean just sex, Izzy. You can't pay the bills—or buy these shoes for that matter—with sex."

"Actually, Phoebs . . . I think you can."

I made sure I had little time to ponder the issue. Activities like working, food shopping, and going to the bathroom became little more than bothersome tasks fit in between hour-long searches on Match.com and JDate.

I was obsessed with the notion that my future husband was lurking somewhere in my computer (though less sure with JDate, where every man was a "mensch" who looked as though he probably was still living at home with his mother) . . . a Jewish knight on a white horse who would gallop up my semicircular driveway and carry me away.

It was as if I had discovered a new career as an anthropologist, schooling myself in the species *Homo divorcicus,* otherwise known as the (mostly) dumped, middle-aged, white male.

I learned about their modes of dress and preferred cocktails. I learned that eloquence via e-mail did not guarantee even a modicum of personal charm. I was often driven to ponder whether a ghostwriter was responsible for the quick wit and lyrical prose, especially on those occasions when the guy sitting in front of me could barely string the words together necessary to order a hamburger.

On the surface, at least, the men were as varied as the myriad restaurants I toured around town. There was the accountant who had lips as big as his face and the lawyer who looked as if he had been wearing his white turtleneck for much longer than was advisable. There was the entrepreneur who shaved his head and bleached his goatee and the actor who gave me one free ticket—only one—so that I could watch him sing and dance on Broadway.

In spite of the almost constant flow of letdowns, near misses, and largish disappointments, I found myself enjoying the dating process. Like working as a waitress without the tips and ketchup stains, dating's best perks were undoubtedly the happy meals, arriving as they did with fine wine and risotto in lieu of a Coke and some fries. Unlike the mostly budget-level assignations of my youth, grown-up dating involved dinners with cocktails and lunches with dessert.

It appeared that in the fourteen or so years since I was last on the hunt, I had somehow morphed from a shy, insecure girl who didn't quite fit into a fearless femme fatale with little time and lots of attitude. I also discovered that I liked men a lot better now that I wasn't so unsure around them. I listened to their stories of wives who, after kids were born and houses bought, realized that they no longer wished to be living with the men they had once loved and married. These men were all, with differing degrees of desperation, searching for the "right woman," convinced that their past failures had given them the secret to getting it right the next time.

And then there was me—having made it through my first marriage with nary a scratch—with little more than a clue of how not to mess it up the second time around. There should be a checklist of what traits to look for, I thought, handed out at the restaurant door. Or at the very least a bell that would sound to signify a suitable match when we looked into each other's eyes after ordering our grande cappuccinos.

Wendy's advice was to withhold judgment before the third date. My own experience—almost rejecting Michael and later

falling for someone as atypical as Charlie—reinforced the logic of
a lengthy "interview" process. Despite the advice, most of my al-
liances were single dates resulting neither in a second meeting nor
in a good-night kiss. The few men I was open to multidating never
seemed to ask.

That was not the initial problem with Larry, a guy I met on
JDate who seduced me with his charm and his summer place on
Long Beach Island ("second house off the water," he crooned).
The first two dates—dinner and a late lunch—were promisingly
low-key. He seemed reasonably well adjusted, well spoken, and
well dressed—on the whole a healthy prospect. During the third-
date dinner of salad and designer pizza, the healthy part of the
deal proved an early and misguided assumption.

"I was quite the stud before my prostate surgery," he told me,
pizza sauce dripping down his chin.

"I bet," I nodded, not quite sure of the proper response to
this type of revelation.

"Not now, though," he added.

I looked up.

"Not now?" What good was a house second off the beach
without a healthy prostate?

"Nope," he said with a sad smile. "Like trying to shove a marsh-
mallow into a piggy bank."

As was inevitable, after a slew of Jeffs and Brads and Stevens,
there was even a guy with the same name as my husband.

"Isn't that weird?" asked my stepson David, the designated
stand-in, since Michael's death, for the girls' school events. He had

taken a bus from his apartment in Queens for Jenna's annual talent show and, arriving early with a large bouquet of flowers, had snagged us second-row seats.

"Not really. I just call him 'hey you.' "

Michael the Second lasted through the spring and into the summer—coming as he did with home-made smoothies and foot massages on demand.

"So *now* what's the problem?" asked Phoebe, exasperated by my batting average.

"Putting aside the fact that he lives with his parents, there just doesn't seem to be any chemistry."

"Thank God for that! Charlie may not have a lot to recommend him, but at least he has his own place!"

So I moved along to Andy, a guy who created and wrote a popular cable TV show.

"How do you know he's not lying?" my sister Wendy asked.

"Because if he was lying he'd say he wrote for *Seinfeld,*" I patiently explained.

Andy seemed like a distinct possibility. He was funny. He was warm. And he had a screening room in his basement.

"He sounds like he may be The Guy," said Charlie over Tuesday night takeout Mexican. "Maybe you two could get married and we could, you know, take turns using the screening room."

"You're kidding me, right?"

He turned me toward him, suddenly serious. "I love you, Isabel. You're the best thing that's ever happened to me. Ever. I only want what's best for you and the kids, and if you think the Cable Guy is it, then we can stop seeing each other and you can give it a shot."

But visions of Charlie in the screening room wouldn't go away, and after a few dates I asked Andy if we could take a hiatus for a couple of weeks as I had another "log" on the fire. When Charlie proved to be a disappointment . . . again, I found that Andy and his screening room had moved on.

"So what number are you up to now?" my mom asked over dessert at a nearby restaurant. She had stopped for an early dinner after meeting a client in New York and was taking advantage of the few minutes we had alone while the kids were in the bathroom.

"What do you mean 'what number'?"

"You know . . . how many men?"

Uh-oh, I thought. "Why do you ask?"

"Well," she said, leaning in confidentially, "I heard somewhere that dating is really just a numbers game. The twenty-eighth guy you meet," she said, "will be the one."

"Really? What about the first twenty-seven?"

"I don't know. Practice?"

"Hmmm. Do I have to date 'em only once? Or do they only count if they're a multiple date?"

"Gee," my mother said thoughtfully, tapping her manicured fingernails on the tablecloth. "I'm not sure."

"And do I have to sleep with the twenty-seven prior to number twenty-eight? Or just maybe dinner?"

"Well . . . maybe dinner and a movie."

"Does coffee count?"

"Jeez, Iz," she said, throwing up her hands. "I don't know!"

I found that Match and JDate, like the rivers and streams in the Midwest, were pretty well stocked when it came to fishing.

Since I had begun the process, I was usually able to schedule at least one date every other week.

The kids bounced noisily back to the table. I pulled a piece of paper from my handbag and made a quick list.

"Let's see . . . there's Charlie, of course. Then John from Jericho, Big Lips, Dirty Turtleneck, Beach House . . ."

"Don't any of these guys besides Charlie have names?"

I ignored the question, trying to remember some of the less-than-memorable candidates. Except for Charlie it was mostly like Oz—they all came and went very quickly.

I added them up.

"OK. The guy I had coffee with last week was number ten."

"Can I draw too, Mommy?" asked Jenna.

"Sure, honey." I handed a piece of paper and a pen to her and Sadie.

"Was he nice?" asked my mother.

"He had a nice smile. But he ended up blowing me off the day before our second date . . . which was OK because I planned to blow *him* off to go to the movies."

"With who?"

"With moi." I dropped my voice and leaned in toward her. "Listen, I may not be up to twenty-eight guys yet, but I *have* realized that a bucket of buttered popcorn and a fountain Coke are often a far more reliable source of enjoyment than a personal injury lawyer with an ex-wife who likes to dress up as a poodle and have sex with the neighbor's Lab."

My mother checked to see if the kids were paying attention before looking at me with a weird combination of horror and interest.

"You're making that up."

"Yeah. I am. But you get the point. Anyway, the guy I had a drink with on Wednesday night was number eleven but he wasn't my type."

"So you're up to number eleven?"

"More or less. But I'm having lunch on Monday with a Protestant Fire Chief, who will be number twelve. And a drink with a guy who looks a little like Will Ferrell on Thursday, who will be lucky number thirteen."

Mom looked up from her slice of Awesome Coconut Cake. "Will Ferrell?"

"Yeah . . . but Will Ferrell in *Kicking and Screaming,* not Will Ferrell in *Elf.*"

"I saw *Elf!*" exclaimed Sadie. "That's the one where the guy eats spaghetti and syrup for breakfast!"

"That's right, honey," I said. I took turns admiring their drawings, still life on placemats, then turned back to my mom.

"So anything beside the elf?" Mom asked, eyebrows arched.

"There's someone in the city I've dated a couple of times. I'm meeting him for lunch on Friday."

"You must like him," she said, fishing, "if you're going all the way into the city to meet him for lunch."

"Actually, Mom, he's more like a friend at this point. And I have to be in the city anyway for a court appearance."

"Please tell me it has nothing to do with the elf."

"Nope. Just a simple moving violation." I had been stopped for making a right turn on red and could produce only a tired smile and an expired insurance card. What I didn't tell my mother, because it sounded a bit deranged, was that I had also made a date with the guy who would be number fourteen—a Jewish pharmacist and father of six from Brooklyn who, due to a shortage of time on my part, had agreed to meet me at the hearing.

"Well, Mom, if you can count just one date—and if a good-night kiss isn't a requirement—by next week I should be up to about fifteen."

"Wow," said Mom, always on hand with an encouraging word. "You're more than halfway there!"

CHAPTER TWELVE

I had read about Dinner Reservations in *The New York Times*. For a fee of five hundred dollars, plus the cost of your meal, two fast-talking former sales reps would arrange three dinner parties at a New York City restaurant with three other women and four carefully preselected men. It sounded like a wedding, except you didn't have to bring a gift or dance the hora.

The day of the first dinner arrived. Dinner Reservations e-mailed me a list of tips, which I reviewed over breakfast after dropping the kids off at day camp. The directives to "Arrive on time for cocktails" and "Turn off your cell phone" sounded pretty routine, but they were immediately followed by the suggestion to "Bring a smile, a joke, and a funny story." Was I being prepped for a singles dinner party or a late-night talk show?

I continued to read down the list. "Clothing should be business casual, call if you're running late, and"—this one was bolded—"conversations should steer clear of prior dating experiences."

"What will you do if they're all losers?" asked Phoebe helpfully.

"You mean if they chew with their mouths open and use the wrong salad fork?"

"I'm serious. It's not like my wedding—you can't switch tables if you hate the people you're stuck with." She dropped her voice. "Especially if it's the *head* table and you're sitting with your new in-laws."

But unlike Phoebe at her wedding, I did have a back-out plan. Ivana, who was watching the kids for the evening, had agreed to call me on my cell phone at precisely eight o'clock. If I was having a lousy time, I'd tell the group that my child was at home puking her guts up and hope that the beefy Dinner Reservations representative would let me out the door.

Surprisingly, considering how long it took me to get dressed in "business casual," I arrived at the restaurant on time and found that two potential suitors had gotten there before me. If not quite gorgeous intellectuals, neither were they drooling idiots. One, a widower with a dimple named Ken, was particularly attentive and quickly grabbed the seat next to mine at the bar. Slowly the rest of the group assembled, made up of a mixture of boroughs, cities, and clothing choices.

When everyone arrived, we sat down at the table—boy, girl, boy, girl. The free cocktail provided by Dinner Reservations helped grease the wheels, and by the time the meal and additional alcohol had been ordered, most of us were chatting like, if not quite old friends, then at least giddy business associates.

I didn't see any conspicuous cell phones or blatant wardrobe mistakes, but Rule Number One—don't discuss past dating experiences—was broken before we finished our appetizers.

"So . . ." relayed Bachelorette Number One, a tall, fortyish blonde with shiny skin. "He arrives at my door—on time and with flowers."

Bachelorettes Number Two and Three, a giggly brunette with big hair and an uptight Wall Street type, respectively, sighed; the men rolled their eyes in unison. Perhaps due to Blonde and Shiny's low-cut polyester blouse, everyone leaned in just a bit as she continued.

"He takes me to the coziest restaurant. He tells me he's been there before and asks me if it's OK if he orders. The conversation flows and the wine he orders—not for nothing—costs two hundred dollars a bottle."

"Old trick," said Bachelor Number Three, a big-faced man with a Brooklyn accent. "He just wanted to get you into bed."

Blonde and Shiny shot him a look. "I got news for you, fella. He didn't need the wine."

Bachelor Number Two, a white-haired gentleman, and Bachelor Number Four, a husky guy with hairy hands, exchanged hopeful glances. Big Face shrugged his shoulders as Blonde and Shiny continued with her story. ·

"So we have some wine . . . a little dinner. And then somehow we get on the subject of past relationships."

"Uh-oh," says Ken, my designated Bachelor Number One.

"I oh-so-briefly skim over my last loser and then he takes the floor. He looks kind of sad. So I ask him what happened. 'Well,' he says. 'Me and Fran were eating dinner . . . just like this. And she says to me, "I'm sorry about your shirts, Lenny. But I didn't get a chance to pick them up at the cleaners." It sounds perfectly innocent to me, so I ask him, 'So what did you do?' And he says, like it's nothing, 'I leaned across the table and I socked her.' "

"Whoa," says Ken, dimples flashing.

I reflected for a moment that while my dating experiences hadn't been all that fabulous, at least thus far I hadn't been socked. And then my cell phone rang and all eyes at the table were suddenly upon me. I had broken Rule Number Two.

I saw Ivana's home number flash on the screen and immediately flipped open my phone. "How is Jenna feeling?" I asked anxiously. To which Ivana replied, "You tell me."

Actually, I was finding that it was nice to be out in the city, sharing war stories over a good dinner with a bunch of interesting grown-ups. So I told Ivana, for the benefit of my tablemates listening in, that I was glad Jenna was feeling better. I asked her to tell the kids that I would come in and kiss them good night when I got home.

And then I went back to flirting with Ken.

But just as with my computer candidates, Ken and I failed to connect. When, after a few e-mails, he disappeared off my radar while fly-fishing in Russia, I paused to take a shallow breath. The next dinner party was at least a month away.

I tried relentlessly to focus on the positive. I was freelancing steadily for a large public relations agency in New York City and had several smaller clients on retainer. Jenna, having started tae kwon do at the ripe old age of three, had just received her black belt. Sadie finally overcame her fear of the water and made it to the deep end of the pool without her swimmies. And although I had come to accept them as nothing more than passionate diversions, there were still my Tuesday nights with Charlie. But still, I couldn't help but feel as if my life had leveled off at not-that-great. Because for me it was still about finding a place where I fit. And as a single mother with two kids living in the suburbs, that meant finding The Guy. And from that perspective, it was beginning to seem that my client's story about how his best friend's wife fell apart the third year following her husband's death was right on the mark.

Things weren't getting any better.

"Don't worry," said my next-door neighbor Ida. "You'll find someone."

She had been divorced once and widowed once and was thoroughly bitter about both experiences.

"And if you don't," her eyes seemed to say, "your life will be like shit."

The specter of ending up alone continued to haunt me. So rather than slowing down to take stock and count blessings, I continued to tally up the prospects and briskly moved along to my next adventure in modern matchmaking.

Speed Dating—a three-minute version of *What's My Line?*—did away with dinner and friendly banter on the assumption that there's very little chance that someone who can't keep you interested for a few short minutes will be scintillating over drinks and dinner, let alone a lifetime. But what Speed Dating lacked in food it made up for in warm bodies. Instead of the mere four potential Romeos at Dinner Reservations, Speed Dating offered up twenty-six.

On a sultry, late summer night in the city, just past the second anniversary of my husband's death, my destination was Pink, the hip downtown bar that was hosting the event. I was greeted at the door by a pretty young girl who asked, in a voice that I thought unnecessarily loud, if I was there with the rest of the losers for the Speed Dating. (She didn't actually say the "loser" part.) This particular event was for men ages thirty-five to forty-five and women thirty to forty. I was almost two years over the event's age limit and hoped that I wouldn't get carded. I could image the headline—*Old Widow Tries to Crash Speed Dating Event!!!*—and was praying that the greeter wouldn't notice the gray peeking out from my temples or the lines that were becoming impossible to hide on my face. I cursed Charlie for suggesting I grow out my bangs. At least the damn things covered my deeply etched forehead.

To my relief the girl barely looked up before wishing me luck and handing me a white "Hi-my-name-is" sticker with the number one on it. Normally I discard these types of things immediately, but the helpful girl said that this was the way any interested men would keep track of me. As if my brilliant smile, sweaty palms, and charming personality were not enough.

After using the bathroom, I got a drink and perched on the arm of a red velvet chair—hoping this was something a thirty-to-forty-year-old woman would do. The space was beginning to fill. Regulars stayed in front by the bar while the Speed Daters, a slightly more anxious-looking group, took their seats at a row of intimate cocktail tables in the back of the room. An endless stream of pretty-couples-in-love passed by outside and, having been alerted to the evening's activities by a billboard-size sign at the front, ogled us as if we were specimens in a singles-only petting zoo.

Precisely three minutes after everyone had found a seat, the greeter from the door blew a whistle, and the men rose as one and moved along to the next empty seat. It was dating Fellini-style with a bit of ring-around-the-rosy thrown in. By the time Bachelor Twenty-Six took his seat—a bow-tied Republican who dutifully listed his assets and only stopped short of supplying his penis size—my eyes were blurry, the whistle was hurting my ears, and I was in serious need of another drink.

"So," I asked Wendy. "Where's the slugger taking you for this year's anniversary?" I was sitting on the edge of her bed while she packed.

"Mets versus Atlanta. Doubleheader.

"Sounds lovely."

"Trust me, after the game it's dinner for two and then a night without kids at a three-star hotel." She flashed me a contented smile.

"Let's just hope they win."

"Oh yes," answered my sister knowingly. "He'll be in a *much* better mood if they win." Wendy folded a few last things in her bag and came over to sit by me. "Arnie and I really do appreciate you watching the kids overnight. You sure you can handle it?"

"Oh, please. Max and Eric keep the girls so entertained, they end up doing all of the work for me. It's no trouble, really."

"Wait till you try to get 'em into bed! Now that school has started again it's almost impossible."

"Speaking of school . . ."

"Yes?" Wendy answered. "Are the girls doing OK?"

I shook my head. "Uh-huh. But I have a question."

"Go on."

"Well . . . what do you think the rules are for dating your kid's friend's dad?"

"Come again?"

"Jenna has a friend . . . nice girl. And the friend has a dad."

"Is the dad married?"

"Not anymore."

"Is he cute?"

"Yeah. But he's totally not my type. He has a tattoo on his left arm that says 'Irish.' "

Wendy stood up and went into the bathroom to gather some toiletries. "Well . . . you thought Michael was half Irish and *he* was your type. What else?"

"Gorgeous blue eyes." I hesitated.

"And?" asked Wendy.

"And he's only got seven fingers."

"So?" Wendy said sensibly. I could hear her rummaging through her bathroom cabinet. "It's not like you're gonna arm-wrestle him," she said above the din. "At least not right away. And besides," she added, her head out the bathroom door, "if you know what you're doing you only need one hand anyway. I say go for it."

"How can I go for it? The guy's got primary custody of four children."

Wendy came back into the room in a rush, her hands full of plastic bottles. "You never said anything about four kids, Izzy. Seven fingers and a tattoo you can deal with. But four kids?"

"He's amazing, Wendy. His refrigerator is spotless. The kids are all well mannered. He's even got them making their own lunches." I stood up and added plaintively, "I can't even get Jenna to school on time!"

"When did you see his refrigerator?"

"I picked up Sadie after a playdate. I asked him how he managed to feed all the kids."

"And?" asked Wendy.

"He told me has a system."

"Jeez, he has a system? Then you *have* to ask him out for a drink," she said, carefully arranging her items in a travel bag.

"When? The only time I see him is when we pick up our kids on the same days, which as close as I can figure are Mondays, Wednesdays, and alternate Thursdays."

"Wow. They've only been in school for a month. You *have* been paying attention."

"I mean, what's the protocol? I can't ask him out in front of the kids. And what if he says *no*? I still have to see him on Mondays and Wednesdays."

"Don't forget alternate Thursdays.

"Well . . . why don't you call him?" Wendy suggested. "He's got a phone, doesn't he?"

I looked up Irish Dad's information in Jenna's class directory, which featured a separate listing for each child. Having fathered four, his number was listed so many times he practically had his own page. I holed up in my bathroom, picked up the phone, and dialed. Jenna's friend answered and, feeling like a nervous teenager, I asked if her father was at home. Irish Dad was matter-of-fact when he answered, perhaps believing I had called to arrange a playdate. When I managed to cough up the real reason, he hesitated just a moment before answering *yes*.

We scheduled to meet for a cup of coffee in between his elder daughter's choir practice, his younger daughter's magic class, his elder son's soccer, and his youngest son's ballet. "What can I tell you?" he said, shrugging his shoulders. "The kid likes to dance."

The conversation centered on our children—giving him a two-kid advantage—and by the end of the date I discovered that Irish Dad was not just missing a few fingers. He was also lacking in anything resembling an interest in me. And really, even if he was interested, where would he find the time?

As if by divine providence, I opened my mailbox one late fall afternoon to find a letter addressed to Single Resident.

Do you really want to spend another holiday alone? it inquired.

No, I thought. I do not.

I ripped the envelope open to find an invitation that offered me fun, romance, and excitement with the Perfect One, all for a nonrefundable and nonspecific fee. I was coming up empty on the Internet, and Sadie, Chanukah wish still unfulfilled, had asked if she could get a dad in lieu of a sixth birthday gift. Stalled at eighteen dates—blind or otherwise—and with no prospects on the horizon, I knew I needed to devise another strategy.

I brought the letter upstairs, where it sat on my desk for a week. On the eighth day I decided that no harm could come from inquiring about the fee. The woman who answered the phone informed me that all would be revealed when I came in to meet my "dream guy facilitator."

"I'll think about it," I told her, not wanting to appear desperate. Two days later she called me back and tried to coax me into the fold, using many of the same methods employed by con artists and fishermen.

"There are *so* many great guys out there looking for someone just like you!"

The bait.

"But you've never met me," I answered. "I could be an ugly, acne-ridden ax-murderer."

"Tosh! You sound wonderful. And what a great sense of humor! I'm telling you, just yesterday I had four handsome guys in here, extremely well-off, just begging me to fix them up!"

Live bait.

In retrospect, which I didn't have the benefit of at the time, it sounded quite unbelievable. But what did I know? The first time I swam around the dating pool my only expenses were suntan lotion and a beach towel. Perhaps, now that fix-ups were a thing of the past, you *did* get what you paid for.

I made the appointment.

I arrived at 9:00 A.M. to find spacious offices decorated in early Greek with lots of drawings of Venus and fiberglass statues of buff, naked men. After a few minutes, which I spent admiring the genitals in the waiting room, a tiny blonde with big hair burst forth and greeted me with sisterly affection. She introduced herself as "another Isabel!" as if that made us somehow related. Then she showed me into a smaller version of the outside office (although the penis on the statue in this room looked somehow larger in the smaller space) and invited me to sit down and tell her about my dream man.

"I'm looking for someone nice who has a decent job, who's been married before, and who likes kids. If he's not so ugly that he doesn't scare the children, so much the better."

She paused a moment from taking notes and gave a little chuckle.

"So," I asked. "How much?"

"We have so much to talk about first! Tell me more about *you.*"

I explained about Michael and the kids. The minutes ticked by while I told her that fix-ups and Internet dating weren't working out and that I hadn't had much luck with Speed Dating or Dinner Reservations either. That my daughter wanted a new daddy and, by God, I was going to get her one!

It seemed as though I had been there for hours discussing my history and listening to Isabel explain how the service worked. Finally she pulled out a book the size and density of the New York City phone directory—her client list—and ponderously leafed through its crammed pages. She eventually found what she was looking for and handed the book to me.

I leaned in a little closer to look.

This is weird, I thought. Why is Brad Pitt signed up with a New Jersey dating service?

She watched me staring. She had me hooked, all right. "He's gorgeous, isn't he?"

"Yeah . . . but isn't he already married and living in LA or something?"

"His name is Adam. I know he looks like a movie star but he's actually a widower from Saddle Brook. Wife died of cancer, I think. All her hair fell out." She touched her own blonde bubble and shivered. "Great guy, two sweet kids. I spoke to him yesterday. He's looking for someone just like you. He's perfect. I can feel it!"

A few moments went by, and I sensed that somehow showing me this guy's picture signaled the finale.

"So how much," I asked for the thirty-fifth time, pointing to the picture, "is Adam going to cost me?"

I had planned in advance on spending no more than three hundred dollars. I had heard that these services gave deals to women—you got bonus points if you had all your teeth and hair—and made up the difference with desperate, homely men. Isabel had already explained that, in exchange for a still unknown fee, I would receive three recommendations. And three guys for three hundred dollars seemed like a reasonably good deal.

So when Isabel smiled and said, *"Thirteen* hundred dollars," I almost fell off my gilded chair. "I'm telling you, Izzy—can I call you Izzy?—it's worth that much *just* to meet Adam!" The giant blonde head swooped toward me again. She looked around as if someone else might be listening. "And listen . . . I'll get you a few extra dates. Just in case you and Adam don't hit it off."

The thought of returning to my apartment empty-handed gave me pause. The thought of returning to Match and JDate made me nauseous. And after all, weren't dating services merely an extension of the old-fashioned neighborhood matchmaker, glo-rified in legend and song as far back as *Fiddler on the Roof*?

I signed on the dotted line while daydreaming about my trousseau.

Images of Adam and me strolling on the beach with the kids, celebrating holidays together, and walking down a flower-strewn aisle filled my head like scenes from a soft porn movie. What's thirteen hundred dollars if it makes my kids happy? I thought.

My first recommendation arrived in my mailbox a month later. When the letter arrived, I saw to my dismay that it was not Adam but a single fifty-five-year-old named Murray. Perhaps, I thought, Adam was in Hawaii with the kids. Or maybe he was busy modeling for the new Calvin Klein underwear campaign. I was willing to overlook the fact that on the enclosed photo Murray looked more like Bob Newhart than Brad Pitt, but the letter said that Murray was single. And since one of my few stipulations had been that the man be widowed or divorced, I immediately called Isabel.

"Oh, Isabel was your *facilitator.* From now on you have to deal with Member Services," said the woman pleasantly. I would soon come to realize that "Member Services" meant anyone who happened to be standing by the phone when it rang. The woman put me on hold and redirected the call.

"Hello? Member Services."

"Hi. My name is Isabel Ackerman and I have a question. Does single mean 'not currently married' or does it mean 'never married,' because I requested someone who's been previously married and if it means 'never married' I'm not really interested."
I figured that with a fee of thirteen hundred dollars, each guy was

costing me over four hundred dollars, and a never-married fifty-five-year-old who looked like Bob Newhart certainly couldn't be worth that much.

The woman asked me to hold while she pulled up my "wish list."

"So sorry," she said, coming back on the line. "Single does mean 'never married.' I'll give your folder back to one of our matchmakers and we'll be sending you out another recommendation shortly."

"Well, not that I'm desperate or anything, but I waited a month for Murray. What exactly does 'shortly' mean?"

"When we find your Perfect One, of course!"

"And will that happen in less than a month? 'Cause you do have my thirteen hundred and all."

"Oh, Isabel," she said disapprovingly. "You can't hurry love!"

I hung up with Diana Ross and waited. And waited. Three weeks later another recommendation finally arrived in my mailbox. It still wasn't the promised Adam, but on paper his background looked a tad better than Murray's. His name was Kevin. He was forty-eight and divorced, and he owned his own business. When he failed to ring after a few days, I called him.

"Hi, Kevin. My name is Isabel. I got your profile from the Perfect One."

"Oh, hi," he said, his voice faint.

"Did I wake you?" I hoped not. It was three o'clock on a Tuesday afternoon.

"Oh no," he croaked. "I just got out of the hospital."

"I'm sorry," I said. "Everything all right?"

"It is *now.* Hadn't been to the bathroom in over two weeks.

Cramps. Nausea. Had to have three feet of intestine removed. *Wicked* blockage."

I hadn't even met the man let alone dated him. And "wicked blockage" definitely fell under the category of *way* too much information.

"Sorry to say I won't be up to dating for a while. I'm still attached to a tube for drainage so my mobility is kind of limited. But if you could wait another month or so, I should be up and around."

I thanked him politely and placed another call to Member Services.

"The man you just sent me can't even go to the bathroom by himself! Don't you have someone who's been married and can poop on his own?"

"You can't expect every date we send you to be perfect," the woman said kindly.

"*Yes! I can!* Your service is called *The Perfect One!*"

"Just because the man had a little surgery doesn't mean he's not the right guy for you."

"Listen," I said, growing impatient. "It's been almost two months since I handed over the cash to that fluffy blonde and I still have not had *one date*! What are you guys doing over there?"

"Very well. I'll get another recommendation in the mail for you shortly." Again with the "shortly."

Two weeks later came Craig. At least, I thought, I was working my way up the alphabet. Craig was forty-seven and divorced, and he worked for a Fortune 500 company. Or at least that's what his profile said.

"I'll be honest with you," said Craig. "I was laid off about six months ago, the unemployment's running out, and I've got alimony and child support. But I'd be happy to go dutch."

Black clouds began to form over my head as I again dialed Member Services.

"The Perfect One," the chirpy lady answered.

"Hi, this is Isabel Ackerman. I'd like to speak to the manager, please."

"Not around. I'm sorry. But let me connect you to Member Services."

Before I could tell her not to bother, I was patched back to Neverland.

"I'd like to speak to the manager, please."

"Oh," she said. *"No one* talks to the manager. You could send a letter, though."

"Doesn't he have an e-mail address?"

"Nope. It has to be mailed."

"OK. Who should I address it to?"

"Manager."

" 'Manager'? That's his name?"

"Ha!" she giggled. "I never said it was a *him!*"

I tried to choke back my anger. "Listen, when I came to your office, Isabel promised me a date with some hunk named Adam . . ."

"Adam. Right. Well, Isabel doesn't work here anymore." She lowered her voice. "She kept trying to date the clients."

I felt as if I had somehow stepped into the New Jersey site of the Twilight Zone.

"Do you know what I do for a living?" I asked her. I heard the sound of papers rustling.

"Says here you're a publisher."

"Publicist."

"Sorry. Publicist. Is there a difference?"

"The difference is that I get newspapers and news programs to write about services like yours. Good things *and* bad things. Do you understand what I'm saying?"

"Not really."

"I want my money back."

She did her best to suppress a laugh. "Ah . . . we don't do that."

"But it's been almost three months. I paid you thirteen hundred dollars, and *I still have not had one date!*"

"Well, really . . . it's not our fault that you haven't liked anyone!"

I hung up the phone, broke a few pencils in half, and sat down to write "the manager" a letter.

Two weeks later, when I got nothing but another Dear Single Resident flyer, I decided to take action. I wrote a pitch to the consumer reporters at the local news broadcasts, telling them my dating service horror story. No response. I was about to give up when I got a call a week later from a producer at FOX News.

"We want to do your story. When can we come over?"

"I don't know." I looked around at my disheveled apartment and caught a glimpse of my messy hair in the mirror. "Next week sometime?"

"No no no. I was talking about *tonight*. We'll tease it on the early news and do the full story at ten. I've got a reporter ready to head over to the dating service now. I'd like to send her over to you after that. Say about seven?"

"OK," I said, my discomfort about being the center of attention crowded out by visions of revenge dancing through my head like so many sugarplums. "Seven will be fine." In under an hour I managed to clean the apartment, fix my hair, throw on some blush, and rehearse my lines. The reporter and her cameraman showed up at 6:55 P.M. and gave the apartment and me the once-over.

"So you say the guy they promised to hook you up with looked just like Brad Pitt?" the reporter asked with professional skepticism.

"Could have been his double!"

After two or three takes she had what she wanted. A week later, so did I when the elusive manager from The Perfect One finally returned my phone call. Although the segment had been seen by hundreds of FOX News viewers throughout the tristate area, she seemed strangely unaware of the TV coverage.

"I'm so sorry, Mrs. Ackerman. Had I been working here when you first signed up, this never would have happened."

"Of course not," I replied. "Now if you could just send me a check."

"I could . . . but are you sure? I've got the nicest guy . . ."

I cashed the check I received from The Perfect One and reluctantly signed up for another three months of Match and JDate. I realized that I had searched New York, parts of Long Island, and most of New Jersey and had already dated or been rejected by those few men I had found interesting.

I was still single, I was still in a hurry, and I was more than ready to try something else.

"So how's the dating going?" Wendy asked.

"You know how it's going. Not very well." It was late. I had one hand on the phone and another wrapped around a pint of Ben & Jerry's.

"Maybe it's not time yet."

"You sound like that lady taxi driver who hung up her mascara and heels at forty-five."

"I don't mean it that way," Wendy said. "I just mean that maybe you're not ready for a relationship yet."

"Now you sound like Charlie."

"Don't be insulting. And even if you were ready, I think you're going about it the wrong way."

"Oh, yeah?"

"Don't take this wrong, Izzy, but you just seem a little . . . desperate.

"I'm not going to try to kid you, Wendy. That's because I am."

"You gotta relax."

"Can I use prescription drugs?"

"Look, I know you've probably heard it before . . . but I don't think stuff like this happens until you let go a little."

"How much is 'a little'?"

Wendy laughed. "OK. A lot."

"That's what I was afraid of."

"Listen, all I'm saying is stop trying so hard. You'll meet someone, you know, when you least expect it."

The trouble was, I was *always* expecting it.

Could my next husband be the guy who just stepped into the

elevator? No? Then how about the guy standing in front of me in the movie line? Or could it possibly be Charlie? Truth was, every guy with a sweet smile and a decent car became a prospect. So really, unless he came dressed in a chicken suit and smoking a cigar, there was no way Cupid was going to catch me unawares.

"I'm not saying to give up hope," Wendy went on, "but you have to learn to just let go."

The problem was no one could tell me how to "just let go."

I was willing.

I just wasn't quite able.

CHAPTER THIRTEEN

I had tried the standard mating practices of fix-ups and prodigious flirting. One day I even hit up the president of a scarf company I had seen on a morning talk show. She was attractive, successful, and when she happened to be making a personal appearance at Saks on a day when I happened to be shopping, I wasted no time in accosting her.

She was helping another customer. I waited politely until she finished and the customer was well out of earshot.

"Can I help you?" she asked with a smile.

I told her that I had seen her on television earlier that morning and that I was a publicist. We chatted about some people we knew in common. And then she asked the question. "Are you looking for something in particular?"

I told her there was a sparkly number that I had seen her

pushing earlier on the morning show. Then I asked her if she knew any nice, single men. If she thought me a total lunatic, she did her best to hide it.

"Well, I'll tell you . . . they don't have the sparkly scarf at this particular store, but I can e-mail you later to let you know where you can find it. As for the nice, single guy . . . well, there, I'm afraid, you're on your own."

So be it. It would not be the first time, I realized, nor would it be the last. I girded my loins and considered my options. Just because I was short didn't mean I had to sell myself that way. It just meant that maybe I would have to try a bit harder—to make a bigger splash. I was only five feet tall. So unless my guy was either very small, had bad posture, or was looking on the ground for loose change, he was never going to find me. Obviously I had to go a few steps farther—and to stand a few inches higher—than the average single girl.

Wendy had told me about a friend who had offered a trip around the world to whoever fixed her up with the man she ultimately married. But I had already hit up my friends, most of whom had come up appallingly empty-handed.

But, I thought, what if I could extend the free trip offer to reach out to *friends* of friends? And what better way to spread the word than by e-mail? E-mail . . . where every day my in-box contained something from my cousin in Florida exhorting me with Hallmark-like poetry to spread the word of love. Or from my mom in Philadelphia, letting me know that I'd be doomed to hell for all eternity if I didn't forward her e-mail to one hundred friends in fifteen seconds. Yes. E-mail would make the perfect engine with which to drive my Lookin' for Love train.

So I wrote a letter—part invitation, part competition. Finalizing the text took four days. Editing the Send list took another two. Even then I wasn't sure. I didn't want to sound, as Wendy had suggested, too desperate. Finally, at exactly 8:30 on a Tuesday morning in April, I closed my eyes, said a prayer, and pushed the Send button.

This is what I sent:

YOU ARE CORDIALLY INVITED TO PLAY "HELP ISABEL FIND A HUSBAND"

THE OBJECT OF THE GAME IS SIMPLE AND THE GRAND PRIZE INCLUDES A TRIP FOR TWO ANYWHERE IN THE WORLD (INCLUDING HOTEL & AIRFARE UP TO $3,000.00). NO JOKE!!

THE CHALLENGE:

FIND ISABEL A HUSBAND

THE REASONING:

* ISABEL'S FRIENDS ARE WONDERFUL PEOPLE
* ISABEL'S FRIENDS MUST BE FRIENDS WITH WONDERFUL PEOPLE
* ONE OF THOSE WONDERFUL PEOPLE HAS GOT TO BE SINGLE OR KNOW A GREAT SINGLE GUY

AND LASTLY . . .

* EVEN IF ONE IS A FABULOUS, ATTRACTIVE WOMAN (SUCH AS ISABEL), IT'S STILL *REALLY* TOUGH TO MEET PEOPLE (ESPECIALLY IN THE SUBURBS)

ISABEL:

* 42 YEARS OLD
* SMART
* FUNNY
* SEXY (PHOTO AVAILABLE)

THE GUY:

* LIVES IN THE NEW YORK/NEW JERSEY/CT AREA
* IS BETWEEN THE AGES OF 40–50 (GIVE OR TAKE
  A FEW)
* HAS A GOOD JOB/CAREER
* LOVES KIDS

PLEASE FORWARD THIS E-MAIL TO YOUR FRIENDS, YOUR
SPOUSE, YOUR PARENTS, YOUR COWORKERS . . .
ANYONE WHO MIGHT BE INTERESTED IN FINDING A
GREAT WOMAN OR WHO MIGHT KNOW SOMEONE WHO IS.
IF ISABEL MARRIES YOUR FRIEND, YOU WIN THE TRIP.
IT'S THAT SIMPLE.

Three minutes after I pushed the Send button I was out the door taking Sadie to school. I didn't look back.

Every year at Jenna and Sadie's elementary school the entire fourth-grade class took a three-day educational trip to the mountains. The trip was funded by the parents of said children buying an inordinate amount of wrapping paper. The destination was a camping establishment located approximately three hours away, due north. At Jenna's request I had signed up immediately to be a chaperone. Unfortunately, it turned out that immediately wasn't fast enough. Evidently Jenna wasn't the only fourth grader nervous about sleeping away for two nights in the mountains without a parent.

The decision whether or not to go on the trip seemed to mark a turning point for Jenna. She was almost ten—a slight, self-possessed child with wise eyes and her father's light-up-your-face smile. She was smart, scared, and undeniably all her own. She had had sleepovers since Michael died, but she had never been so far away from Sadie and me for more than one night. She was torn. Practically the whole class would be going. Could she make it on her own with just Daddy's pillow and Mystic, her stuffed dog, for company?

We made a deal. If Jenna wanted to give it a try, I promised to drive up on the second day with Ivana, whose son Austin would also be going on the field trip, to visit. With a slight quiver in her voice, Jenna agreed.

And so it followed that after I sent my *Help Isabel Find a Husband* e-mail and dropped Sadie off at school, Ivana and I headed up to the mountains. I arrived at noon to find Jenna looking relaxed and happy. We ate hamburgers and fries in the log cabin commissary and learned how pioneers made soup. Then Ivana and I headed back home around three.

When Ivana pulled the car over for gas just outside the campgrounds, I picked up my cell phone to call my home machine for messages. There were six of them, the first from Wendy.

"Please, Izzy," her voice pleaded, "tell me you didn't *actually* send out this e-mail."

Despite the fact that she was my sister, Wendy was not one of the people I had run my idea by. I had a feeling her reaction would be something like this, and hearing it live and in color brought back my uncertainty. Perhaps it *was* a stupid thing to do.

Before I could sweat too much over Wendy's response, the second message played. This one was from Corky, a casual friend who also happened be an editor at the *New York Daily News.* Despite the fact that there was a war raging and an election coming up, he said he thought my story would make a nice item for the paper.

And so as Ivana drove south toward civilization—past small towns, grazing cows, and rotting barns—I discussed my recent social history with Corky, explaining about Michael, about Sadie wanting a daddy, and about my dating experiences thus far.

"So," he asked finally, "what is it that you're looking for in a man?"

If I were being honest, I would have told him that I was looking for someone who had looks like George Clooney and assets like Bill Gates. But being heedful of how that might sound to the newspaper-reading public, I went in another direction.

I lied.

"Well . . . as long as he's a nice guy who likes kids . . . looks and money don't really matter."

When I got home there was a call from Corky telling me how well everyone thought the interview went.

"But here's the thing," he added. "We want to take a photo."

"A photo?"

"Yeah . . . and it's got to be sexy. This is the *Daily News,* not

The New York Times. Over here you're competing with Pamela Anderson's cleavage."

The photographer arrived at nine o'clock the following morning, but the sight that met him bore no resemblance whatsoever to a *Baywatch* babe. Sadie had woken at 5:00 A.M. and didn't stop throwing up until well after *Sponge Bob* started two and a half hours later.

Tired, smelly, and drained, I ended up putting on a pair of jeans, a v-neck black shirt (cleavage, cleavage), hoop earrings, a pair of mules, and a prodigious amount of under-eye cover-up.

After snapping a few pictures in my hallway, the photographer suggested moving things outside. I sat down on one of the hard wooden benches and tried to look seductive, while Sadie, obviously feeling better, leapt around the vast yard with the photographer's giant light reflector.

Click.

"Look!" squealed Sadie, "I'm the Tin Man!"

"Over here, Isabel," directed the photographer from behind his camera.

Click.

"Look! I'm a flying saucer! I'm a giant silver Frisbee!"

Click.

It was my first picture in memory where I didn't have to fake a smile.

It was Good Friday and the kids were off from school. My plan was to remain in bed for as long as humanly possible. The phone ringing at 6:52 had not figured into my plan.

"Hello?"

It was Jordan and he was shouting something about the newspaper.

"You're on page three!" he yelled. "Isabel A. Three-quarters of a page and a photo . . . right behind Britney!"

I squinted in the direction of the clock.

"Jordy . . . it's not even *seven*. What the hell are you talking about?"

"I'm on my way to work," he said. "Not everyone can stay in bed till nine, ya know . . . even if it *is* Good Friday. I picked up the paper when I stopped for my grande, half-caff, half-regular. I get it in a venti cup. I like a lot of *leche*."

"What the hell is 'leche'?"

"It's 'milk' in Spanish. Jesus, Isabel, you are *so* white."

I grabbed another pillow and propped myself into a not-quite-sitting position.

"I thought all those coffee stores were faux Italian. And why the hell can't you just say milk? You live in Manhattan, for God's sake. Not Barcelona!"

"La la la. I can't hear you."

"Forget la la la. Tell me what the paper says. And how's the picture?"

"Slow down, Sally. The picture is great. The headline says 'Find me a hubby and I'll send you on a dream trip.' "

"I hope there's some fine print indicating there's a limit, 'cause for three thousand dollars it'll have to be a very little dream."

"Forget about the fine print, Izzy. And listen, if you get anyone looking for a cute, young gay guy, you be sure to pass him on to me."

I reached for the bottle of Poland Spring on my night table and took a swig.

"What happened to Zack from Match?"

"He dumped me."

"His loss."

"Go *on.*"

Pause.

"No, really. Go *on.*"

"I would, honey, but I don't have the energy required right now to sing your praises."

I had known, of course, that I would be in that day's *Daily News.* But even with the photo, I figured it would end up as a small item on page 47, somewhere between the obits and the auto ads. I certainly had not expected to find myself plastered across page three right behind an unflattering front-page picture of Britney Spears. Perhaps, as an experienced PR woman, I shouldn't have been surprised. But I'd been pitching stories for over ten years and I had never, ever gotten anything so stupid on three-quarters of a page, so close to the front of a newspaper. Let alone a New York City newspaper with a daily circulation of over eight hundred thousand.

So much for sleeping late. I said good-bye to Jordan and put on my slippers. I assumed that the paper had probably hit the street a couple of hours before, but, as I booted up my Dell, I was totally unsure of what I would find in my in-box. I held my breath, opened my mail, and watched as the messages multiplied before my still blurry eyes. Thirty-five e-mails, and it wasn't even 7:45!

To my surprise, the first several messages were *not* from hopeful suitors, or even from strangers trying to collect on the trip. They were, instead, from hopeful news outlets.

"We want you to be on *The Early Show!*" proposed the first producer.

"How'd you like to do a phone interview on our radio program!" read another.

Since my intention had been to find a nice single man and not a place on Jay Leno's couch, I skimmed the ten or so e-mails from the news outlets and moved on to the actual responses. These ranged from "Marry me and I'll make you happy" to "I have a friend who'd be perfect for you and, p.s., I've always wanted to visit Jamaica." To be fair, there seemed to be just as many responses from people who said they didn't want the trip . . . just to meet a nice woman or to see a single friend happy.

Most of the e-mails were well written and deeply felt. There were notes entreating me to "Leave things in the Lord's hands" and to "Accept your fate and devote the rest of your life to charitable service." There were pleas from taxi drivers, proposals from accountants, and a communiqué from a supervisor from the New York City Department of Sanitation whose screen name was Psycho. I read through thirty-two e-mails. And even though I was sitting safely in my living room in a long-sleeved T-shirt and Victoria's Secret leggings, I still felt downright naked.

I pulled the shades and began typing.

"Thanks for the good wishes," I replied to the well meaning. For those who sounded like possibilities (correct spelling, no criminal record), I asked for a photo. As quickly as I sent them out, new e-mails poured in.

It suddenly dawned on me that if only *one* percent of the *Daily News* readership responded, that would still total well over eight hundred e-mails. How would I sort through them all? And even with my bountiful dating experiences, would I be able to tell from a snapshot and a couple of paragraphs if a man was the psychotic or right guy for me?

The kids woke up an hour later to find me pale, bleary-eyed, and crouched over my keyboard.

"I thought you didn't have to work today," said Jenna.

"I don't."

"Then why are you sitting in front of your computer?" asked Sadie, "and why do you look so funny?"

Good question. Overwhelmed, I immediately put in a call to Phoebe, who Good Friday be damned, was also busy at work.

"All these news shows want to interview me."

"You're kidding. Why?"

"Go get a copy of today's *Daily News*. Page three."

"Page three?"

Phoebe called for her assistant to bring her a copy of the paper. I heard some rustling. Then, "Oh my God, Izzy! You look fabulous!"

"You really think so?"

"Love the shoes!"

"Thanks. But what about the news shows?"

"Do 'em all!"

"What do you mean 'Do 'em all'? *National* broadcast outlets want me to go in front of a camera and tell the world I'm lonely and looking for a husband!"

"Well, you are, aren't you? Hey . . . you think you can bring a friend?"

"I thought you had sworn off men for a while."

"I said for a while. I didn't say forever."

"Phoebe!"

"Sorry."

"Oh my God!" I said, the reality of it slowly dawning. "What will my in-laws think?"

"Forget about your in-laws! *Call those producers and tell them you're in.*"

"But Phoebe . . . I'm shy!"

"You weren't so shy when FOX News came calling."

"That was different. There was money at stake."

"So now it's love. Get over it."

I didn't think I could. What had started out as a lark was quickly growing to nightmare proportions. There was a reason I spent my professional life making other people famous. Perhaps it was a lifetime of being overlooked because of my diminutive size, but I was a behind-the-camera kind of gal. I could tell you what to say and how to say it . . . just as long as I didn't have to say it myself.

I hung up the phone and stared at my computer screen. Forty-one e-mails, forty-two . . .

"I thought we're going to Aunt Wendy's today," said Jenna, arms folded tightly in front of her.

"We are, we are."

"Not if you don't get off the computer!" complained Sadie.

They were right. It was a holiday and we had planned to spend the day together. I had not figured page three in the *Daily News* into that plan.

Half an hour and sixty more e-mails later we were dressed and ready to sit down for breakfast. The phone rang again at 9:15.

"Don't answer it!" yelled Sadie.

"I have to get it. It could be work."

Liar, I thought. A little taste of fame and now you're lying to your children.

It was my mom.

"Regis! Regis!" she was yelling.

"No. It's Isabel. Your daughter. Who's Regis?"

"*Regis and Kelly*! The show! They just held up the newspaper with your picture in it!"

"Get *out*!!!"

In the years since Michael had died, watching television had become a forsaken treat—kind of like Raisinettes and ice-cream sodas. It wasn't a quality issue but rather a paucity of time. The only occasion on which this was not a problem was three mornings a week between 9:00 and 9:30 when I happened to be walking on a treadmill at the gym while happily watching *Live with Regis and Kelly*. So it was with great alacrity that I ran to my television.

"Hey! What about *Sponge Bob*?" demanded Sadie as I grabbed for the remote.

Evidently I didn't run fast enough, as Kelly and Regis had already moved on to weightier topics. I was heading back to the table to finish my oatmeal when the phone rang yet again.

"Is this Isabel A.? Manless in Montclair? The woman in today's *Daily News*?"

"That depends. Who's this?"

"My name is Patty Lane. I'm a producer at *The Early Show*."

"Hi, Patty. How'd you get my phone number?"

"Just did a little research. I hope you don't mind."

It wasn't so much that I minded. But I was getting increasingly freaked-out at how easily everyone but my perfect man seemed able to track me down.

"I loved your story—what a great way to meet a guy!—and we'd like to have you as a guest on the show."

"Mmmm, not sure, Patty. Can I think about it and get back to you?"

As I hung up the phone, I happened to glance at the computer, where up popped an e-mail from CNN. Great, I thought, it's not enough that I've gone national. Now I'll have guys e-mailing me from Pakistan. Included in the message was a phone number. I called.

"We'd possibly want to do something on your story for the lifestyle portion of our evening news show."

"When?"

"Today."

"But I'm leaving in a few minutes for my sister's house in Doylestown."

"Doylestown . . . Ohio?"

"No. Pennsylvania."

"No problem! We could meet you down there!"

The thought of CNN setting up cameras amid multiple children at Wendy and Arnie's house made me chuckle. But I seriously needed some time to think about the sudden onrush of unwanted attention.

I declined.

I did, however, feel obligated to check in with Corky, who had asked me to let him know what kind of responses I was getting.

"Let me put it this way," I told him. "There are a *lot* of single guys out there who read the *Daily News.*"

"That's great! Listen, we'd like to do a short follow-up story in tomorrow's paper. Maybe it'll narrow the field if you tell me *exactly* what you're looking for."

I grabbed on to the "narrow the field" comment and gave Corky a short list.

"Preferably Jewish, loves kids, forty to fifty years old, 5'8" to 5'11". And a good speller."

I needed to eliminate, to find something, anything, to help me figure out who might be a possible match.

By the time we left for Wendy's at 10:30, I had over one hundred e-mails. I grabbed the kids and fled.

I ran into Ivana on the way out the door.

"All hell has broken loose!" When I explained what was going on, she smiled and said, "Life . . . it's just *amazing*!"

Evidently there were other reporters who didn't mind doing a little research; my cell phone continued to ring during most of the drive to my sister's. The saving grace was that Wendy's house was off the beaten track, and once I was ensconced there, my phone couldn't pick up a signal. Sure, I could have turned it off. But it was like a car accident—I couldn't look away.

When the kids went out to play after lunch, Wendy and I had a few minutes to talk.

"This is nuts," I said, picking at a cookie while seated in her kitchen. "I don't know what to do."

"Look . . . you know I haven't quite agreed with your methods, but what the hell . . . What's done is done. Make the best of it."

"That's not advice, Wendy. In fact it sounds a whole lot like a John Denver song."

"OK . . . so how's this? Read the e-mails, make a few dates and . . . what the hell, Izzy." She slapped the table for emphasis. *"Get out there and find yourself a husband!"*

Saturday dawned — just as Friday had—a little too early for my taste.

"Are you crazy?" asked Phoebe, having read the *Daily News* follow-up story, also on page three. "It says that the guy's got to like Bill Maher!"

"So? I love Bill Maher. And besides, it's shorthand for saying I'm looking for a smart liberal with a wicked sense of humor who believes in homeopathic medicine and gay marriage."

"This is the *Daily News*, Izzy. Not *The New York Times*. Half the readers are going to think you're looking for a *threesome.*"

It seemed that the other half of the readers assumed I was in one helluva hurry or possibly in need of a green card. Only weeks after the story appeared, and before I had even scheduled a single date, I was receiving e-mails asking if I was, perchance, *still* available.

Thankfully, breaking news preempted my scheduled television appearances, but still, as a result of the *Help Isabel Find a Husband* e-mail and the follow-up *Daily News* story, I received over eight hundred e-mails by mid-May. My daily routine now consisted of dropping the kids off at school, putting in an hour at the gym, grocery shopping, public relations work, a little laundry, cleaning, and—prior to picking up the kids at school—answering every sin-gle response that found its way into my e-mail in-box. Phoebe's assistant offered to help me sort it out, but, like washing dirty un-derwear or applying mascara, it felt like a job I should do myself.

After a month of reading and responding, I winnowed the eight hundred e-mails down to ten possibilities. Of those ten, after a preliminary phone call, I made plans with five. One of the poten-tials was dating a married woman at the time and thought it best not to further complicate things. I agreed with him.

Obviously my selection process had a few bugs.

Candidate Number One was named John. After the requisite back-and-forth e-mails—foreplay for the modern age—we decided to meet for lunch in the city. I went alone, although Corky had playfully suggested the possibility of following discreetly behind to take notes.

John and I had decided to meet at a restaurant in Rockefeller Center at noon. I arrived on time and watched the tourists as I con-templated my fate. Would John, number twenty-one in my dating pantheon, be the One? He arrived at twelve on the nose, wearing a navy turtleneck that complemented the blue in his eyes and the gray in his hair. He held out his hand and took mine in a firm grip.

John had quite an advantage, I reflected, having read about my life's history on page three of his daily newspaper. I wasn't quite sure where to start, as this scenario was even more peculiar than Internet dating had been.

"You're divorced, right?" I asked.

"Yeah . . . about three years now."

I didn't want to pry, but I did feel the need to—informationally at least—catch up.

"Why'd you break up?"

"It was Father's Day. My wife and kids served me breakfast in bed and presented me with a two-hundred-dollar gift certificate to Home Depot. It was a nice day and my ex suggested that I take the kids and go pick something out. But when we got to the store I realized I had left the gift certificate at home. When we got back, I found her in bed with our neighbor."

And they say war is hell.

By the time dessert arrived, it was fairly obvious that there was no chemistry between us (although the cheesecake was outstanding). John picked up the check, but not before asking if it was all right that he paid.

"Of course it's all right," I said, thinking that we must have run up quite a tab. "Are there actually women who say it's not?"

"These days," he said somewhat wearily, "you never know."

Candidate Number Two arrived at our date with a black eye and two missing teeth. He didn't explain why, and frankly, after hearing him go on for an hour about his life in podiatry, I no longer cared.

Dates three and four were less bruised, but there was little chemistry.

The e-mails continued to dribble in, but my enthusiasm was fading fast.

CHAPTER FOURTEEN

"I think you should kill 'em."

"Huh?"

I had decided to hire a personal trainer when I figured that Michael's beyond-the-grave cheerleading could use some on-the-ground backup. So one morning a week I spent an hour at the gym, working out with Jeffrey, a 6'2" coffee-colored man with a shaved head, rippling muscles, a trim mustache, and large puppy-dog eyes.

We were at the bicep machine, and I was attempting to do twelve reps at thirty-five pounds.

"For the next *Daily News* article," Jeffrey replied. "How long do you think people are going to be interested in a sad, sappy story about a middle-aged—"

Lift. Lift. Lift. Stop lifting.

"I beg your pardon?"

"NO ONE IS GOING TO BE INTERESTED—"

"OK. I heard you. And what makes you think there's going to be a 'next' article?"

"You said that the paper was interested in what happens next. Of course that might change if you don't spice things up a bit. No one's going to be interested—"

"OK. I got it, I got it. Spice it up how?"

"Well, I say you snap." Jeffrey raised his large left hand and snapped his fingers. "You've been dating all these losers and they've been treating you like shit."

"Actually," I said, finished with biceps and moving on to tris, "they've all been pretty nice." I adjusted the seat on the weight machine and thought back over my twenty-something dates, probably more than twice the men I had dated the first time I was single.

Jeffrey roused me from my endorphin-powered reverie.

"Come on, Izzy. Don't you want to be a celebrity?"

"No." I began my next round of reps.

Lift. Lift. Lift.

"OK," Jeffrey said, "think about it this way. You did this for a reason, right? To find your kids a daddy. You can't stop now."

Actually, I was feeling the burn and would have preferred to. "I can't?"

"Shit, no! But you got to keep it interesting if you want them to keep writing. Give 'em what they want!"

"What do they want?"

"Drama! Body parts! Blood and guts!"

"This is supposed to be a warm and fuzzy story, Jeffrey. Not *Dawn of the Dead.*"

But Jeffrey was on a roll. "Think Sharon Stone in *Basic Instinct*. Think Hamlet's mom. Mean! But instead of using a knife to knock 'em off, you use, maybe, a frying pan."

"A frying pan?"

"Yeah, a frying pan. You make 'em buy you dinner. Invite 'em up for coffee. Then when they're admiring your etchings, it's BANG . . . straight to the head!" Jeffrey looked me up and down. "You've been working out. And if you're strong enough to bench-press fifty pounds, then you sure as hell can kill someone with a frying pan."

The middle-aged woman standing next to me channeling Jennifer Beals in *Flashdance* dropped her five-pound weight. I looked away from her and back at him.

"You're crazy."

"Don't you *want* someone to buy your story and make it into a movie?"

"A movie?"

"Yeah. A movie. With Demi Moore as you."

"Demi Moore?"

"Yes. Demi Moore."

Lift. Lift. Stop lifting.

"Can she wear a bikini? I mean, can Demi Moore play me in a bikini? Because if she'll be me in a bikini then I'll be happy to grab a frying pan and kill every one of those bastards!"

"Yes," he said with a dimpled smile. "She can wear a bikini."

"So how many you up to now?" quizzed my mom, as she did every time we had a telephone conversation, referring to what I now thought of as the magic-meet-a-guy talk-show number.

"Twenty-four, I think."

"Jeez, I thought for sure the *Daily News* ad would have put you over the top."

I had spent a good part of my professional life trying to explain to people the difference between public relations and advertising. This time it was personal.

"Actually, Mom," I told her, not for the first time. "It wasn't an ad."

"Well . . . ," she said. "It wasn't much of a *news* story." This from a woman who got all her hard news from *People* magazine.

"It *was* for the *Daily News!*"

Despite my desire to see where it led, the *Help Isabel Find a Husband* interview process began to feel more like work than it did an adventure. "Tell me more about yourself," these quantities of unknown men politely asked. *More about myself?* It already felt as if I had bared enough to eight hundred thousand New Yorkers to last me a lifetime. And whatever there was left to tell, I was tired of squeezing it in between the time I had left after playing with my kids, earning a living, cleaning my apartment, and keeping my quickly graying hair glowing with natural-looking blonde highlights.

When I arrived at Phoebe's one night for dinner and saw page three stuck to her refrigerator, I felt more nausea than pride. The truth was I just wasn't comfortable being in the spotlight, and although I didn't quite feel violated, I did feel a teeny bit transgressed.

It may have been worth the embarrassment, I thought, had

my fame been hard won. But it seemed unwarranted for something as senseless as young widowhood and a child's wish for a new daddy. I was a publicist, and I knew the *Daily News* story for what it really was—a great product placement, but a product placement nonetheless.

"You've got to keep going," said my mom.

"But I'm tired. I don't feel like sorting through any more e-mails."

I didn't feel like making any more coffee dates at the local Starbucks with men who passed faster than the bitter coffee. I was out of breath and ready to stop running. Like a four-year-old who had spent most of the day at the playground, I was ready for a cookie and a nap.

"But you're so close!" my mother pleaded.

"I'll let you in on a little secret, Mom. The only thing I'm close to right now is a nervous breakdown."

It wasn't fun. It had become a chore. I was beginning to realize that being alone didn't have to mean being lonely.

Perhaps . . . after all . . . I had gone about this thing all wrong.

It was Tuesday night and, as per my custom, I was eating pizza and salad standing up in Charlie's kitchen. He had been passed over yet again for a computer programming job he was sure he had, the call coming just an hour before the pizza delivery.

I was distractedly picking through the Insalata Caprese while Charlie mixed himself a Belvedere martini.

"I'm sorry about the job," I told him, sucking on an olive pit.

"That's OK. At least I still have you, baby."

I had not sent Charlie the *Help Isabel Find a Husband* e-mail. I knew that he wouldn't outright disapprove, but I thought that he, like Wendy, might find it a little desperate. I also knew—because he rarely read the paper or watched anything but CNN—that if I didn't tell him about it he would never find out. But now that the whole misadventure was winding down, I felt the need to come clean.

"Wait a minute," he said, reaching for my pizza crust. "You're telling me you were on page three of the *New York Post*?"

"The *Daily News*."

"Is there a difference?"

"Yeah . . . the *Post* has a higher circulation."

"It's funny, I think Paul e-mailed me about it."

I had met Paul, Charlie's only friend, once, at Charlie's apartment, and I assumed he must have recognized me from the picture.

"So, did you read the story?"

"Nah . . . I just deleted the e-mail."

"You weren't even curious?"

In our earlier days together, I believed Charlie to be enigmatic. Only lately did I realize that what I took for complexity was actually just selfishness. The only thing that really concerned Charlie was Charlie. As long as I was somewhere in his orbit I was important. Otherwise I was just a piece of flotsam . . . off the radar and incidental.

But still, I made excuses. He canceled plans because he had never experienced the joy of togetherness. He resisted commitment because he didn't want to fail at another relationship. I justified all of his transgressions, whether stupid or hurtful, rather than admit that the man who had saved me in that first horrible year was a jerk. Or at the very least someone who had problems far bigger than mine. Of course he had always said there was no commitment. But it was hard to believe that, after all we had been through together, when push came to shove he would let me walk away.

"Not really curious about the story," Charlie said, his voice becoming cool. "It was, after all, the *Daily News*. But I would like to know how you keep all those responses straight. Do you have a flow chart? Or has Apple developed software that helps you keep track?" He took a sip of his Belvedere before adding, "You really should have come to me, you know. I could have upgraded you to Datetracker Pro."

Was he jealous? Or just pissed off that I hadn't told him sooner? And why did his inability to express his feelings always lead to my heart landing in a bloody heap on his linoleum floor?

"You can't have it both ways, Charlie. You can't be outraged lover and pom-pom girl all at the same time."

"What's that supposed to mean?"

"It means pick a side. Commit."

But either he couldn't or he wouldn't. So he came down somewhere in the middle with an extra dollop of sarcasm.

"How have the dates been?" he asked. "Up to your standards, I hope?"

"I haven't met anyone," I told him flatly.

"Really? With a full-page ad on page three?"

"It wasn't an ad."

"You can't kid a kidder, Isabel." He smiled. "It may as well have been."

"Charlie."

"If dogs run free . . . ," he said.

"What the hell does that mean?"

"It's a Dylan song."

"And?"

"Come on, Izzy, what did you expect? Do you really think your Prince Charming reads the *Daily News*? And if he did, do you think he's going to send you a 'let's run off together' e-mail and a bunch of yellow roses?"

Perhaps Phoebe had called it after all. Perhaps Charlie *was* just like James Dean's invisible squirrel—I could see him and hold him, but in the end he was never really there.

"Charlie?"

"Yeah?"

"I don't think this is working anymore."

"The pizza?"

"No. Not the pizza."

He looked at me with that penetrating gaze of his. "I met you," he said, "less than a year after your husband died. You were frantic. And lonely."

His lips, I thought. I would so miss those lips. My attention began to drift.

"Isabel!"

"Yeah?"

"I'm not stupid, Izzy. I knew there was a pretty good chance I'd end up being your transition guy."

"You didn't have to be. I was ready to commit, Charlie. You know that."

"Yeah. I know," he said softly.

"Then why?"

"Because, my little kumquat, sooner or later you would have wanted a guy with a big, fat paycheck who could buy you fancy stuff and take you fancy places. That's not me. You know that." He laughed. "I'm just a saxophone-playing, cave-dwelling, unemployed drinking man."

I'm not quite sure how, but when he said it, it sounded almost sexy.

I knew ending it with Charlie was the right thing to do. And if by that point I hadn't figured it out, there were legions of family and friends lined up who would have been happy to tell me so. But I was also realizing—with dawning alarm—that now I didn't just need someone to fill Michael's place in my heart. I also needed someone to fill the hole left by Charlie.

"The key," said Ivana, "is to find the strength within yourself. I know you may not *want* to do it on your own. But you should be fully *able* to."

Maybe. But not quite yet.

The holidays were approaching, and everywhere I looked I saw two-parent families and happy couples celebrating. They celebrated on television, in print ads, and in living color at my kids' school. I had a month before Chanukah, and I was determined to be one of them.

"Look," I said to Phoebe via cell phone from Toys "R" Us. "You're a talk-show producer, right? You've got credentials."

"Yeah. So?"

"So maybe I could be your assistant."

"What do you mean? You already have a job."

"I know. But I thought that we could do something fun together! You know . . . maybe rent a video camera and do some kind of documentary thing!" By this point my voice was so high from trying to generate enthusiasm that I could see the GI Joe with the kung fu grip actually flinch.

"What are you talking about, Izzy? What kind of 'documentary thing'?"

"Well, I dunno," I said, moving toward the Barbie aisle. "Maybe a little research on young single doctors in the tristate area. I could do the interviewing and . . ."

"Are you serious?" Phoebe asked. "First you take out an ad in the *Daily News*—"

"It was NOT AN AD!"

"And now this? Who's gonna pay for it? We'd have to get a camera and then we'd have to hire a camera guy. And where would you find these young single doctors? Is there a 'young-single-doctors' directory somewhere that I don't know about? And what if you don't end up meeting anyone? Or even worse . . . you could end up with a plastic surgeon who talks you into extensive surgery—not just Botox but a face-lift, too—and you can't resist 'cause it's free."

"OK, OK . . . never mind! I guess it was a silly idea."

"Look, Izzy," said Phoebe gently. "I know you miss Charlie. And Michael. And you know I'm all about getting out there and going for what you want. But it's not like you're dying, Isabel—you're just single. Truthfully, I don't even know why you *want* to find another guy. Charlie is clearly a loser. And Henry—I don't have to tell you—was even worse. At a certain point I think you have to take a breath." Phoebe paused, taking a breath. "I think it's time, my friend, to sit on the bench and wait it out for a while."

"Wait?" I said, eyes fixed on the deluxe Barbie and Ken Newlywed collection complete with shiny red convertible. *"Wait for what?"*

But when the answer finally came, it was not the one I had been expecting.

Over two years after their father died, Jenna and Sadie finally made the transition back to their own beds, finding that even on a king-sized mattress space was getting tight. The crowding was partly due to my failure to enforce the "no-more-than-two-stuffed-animals-at-a-time" rule. Despite my request to the contrary, the girls took to smuggling in extra "friends" like contraband through customs, creating, by morning, a fluffy free-for-all.

But with every season comes a change. The bedtime routine now consisted of my lying first with Jenna and then with Sadie, catching up on the news of the day. Their sheets were cool; their hair smelled of lavender. Before I left their room each night, we said our prayers, a few lines that Michael had made up with Jenna what seemed like a century ago.

"Dear God," recited my oldest daughter with unnerving gravitas. "Thank you for today and all of our wonderful family and friends."

Sadie, curled up under the covers with one hand wrapped around a piece of my hair, piped up with her new addition, "and a-*nee*-mals."

"And animals," Jenna and I duly repeated.

Then, "We miss you and we love you."

And then came another of Sadie's additions—this one having

appeared sometime last Christmas—"and we wish for a daddy and husband just like you."

"That's not altogether likely," I told her, not for the first time.

"The man *might* be like Daddy . . ." started Sadie.

"But then again," added Jenna. "He may not."

"And perhaps," I added, considering the possibility for the first time, "there may not be another man at all."

"May not be another man?" Sadie repeated, sitting up and throwing a small arm to her forehead in mock horror.

"Well . . . maybe not."

"I'm not sure I want another daddy," Jenna whispered from her bed.

"How could you not want another daddy?" Sadie asked her older sister.

Then Jenna, wise beyond her years, pointed out something so obvious that I couldn't believe I had never really thought of it before. "Because it'll be weird having a stranger live here. And besides," she added, "I'm not sure I want another change."

"Well . . . it's not like he'd drop from the sky or anything," I told them. "By the time he got here—if he did—he really wouldn't be a stranger anymore."

But still, being stuck in the fantasy, I had never actually thought about the day-to-day of it. A man who would have to start at the beginning—map in hand—while the rest of us were already edging toward the middle. A man who wasn't there when my kids were born, when their teeth were lost, when they took their first steps.

We had morphed, as we had to, into a household of three women. Our topics of conversation tended more toward clothes than catch. I alone stood in for Santa and the Tooth Fairy. I offered advice and encouragement and enough love, I hoped, to compensate for an absent daddy. I may have been alone, I reflected, but thanks to my extended friends and family, I was very rarely lonely. Up until that moment I had concentrated on the gauzy, sugar-coated images of once again being a family.

I hadn't realized that, on our own, we already had become one.

How would I ever find a man who could be part of that? And now, after all we had come through, did I still really want to?

CHAPTER FIFTEEN

Nearly two months had passed since I had checked my dedicated *Daily News* e-mail address. It had not been a conscious pause. I was busy with work, the kids, the impending holidays. Somehow finding a man had fallen to the end of my to-do list, right between getting laser hair removal and new floor mats for the car. But Corky called to see what was new, so I figured I'd log in and take a look. Some junk mail had managed to get through—those jack rabbit vibrators again—along with a few notes asking if the free trip and I (in exactly that order) were still up for grabs. I responded that I was indeed still single and that for the moment I was surprisingly happy to stay that way.

Then I noticed a short message dated a few weeks before.

"Your endeavors brought a nice smile. Good luck and try to

stay grounded. As a publicist I'm sure you'll know how to handle."
It was signed, simply, Jack.

Most of the eight hundred or so people who had contacted me as the result of the *Daily News* story had wanted something—the trip, a wife, the chance to save my immortal soul. It was nice to have someone *offering* something, even if it was just a little advice, rather than looking for what he could take away.

I thought for a moment, sitting at my desk, a picture of Michael looking pensively in my direction. And then I composed a response.

"Thanks for the nice note and sorry it took so long to get back to you. Despite your vote of confidence I'm finding that my training as a publicist doesn't seem to cover this type of situation. My original objective—to meet a nice guy—somehow mutated into *What's My Line?*. The morning shows wanted me to talk about my private life, the news shows wanted to follow me around on dates, and my family and friends began treating me like Britney. It felt very strange. Best, Isabel."

Jack's response came back early the next day: "I think it was Thomas Wolfe who once said, 'You have reached the pinnacle of success as soon as you become uninterested in money, compliments, or publicity.' "

Possibly, I thought, but then I'd be out of a job.

"I realize," Jack went on, "that this is unsolicited advice from a stranger, but you may want to take a minute to step back and recoup."

"Actually," I wrote Jack, "I have stepped back. *Way* back. Don't take this personally, but I've come to believe that finding a nice guy via e-mail is like searching for the Holy Grail in a blindfold. It may be doable, but I'm tired of scaling the high walls and fighting the fire-breathing dragons necessary to succeed. Best, Isabel."

"High walls? Fire-breathing dragons? Tell me, Isabel, how many men have you dated in your single diaspora, wandering through the desert of unhappy, single men? I should probably confess up front that I don't really believe in Internet romance—it seems kind of . . . backward. But if you *do* find someone you feel a connection with, it's probably better to enjoy it without a reporter hanging over your right shoulder. Regards, Jack."

What started as a three-line compliment quickly developed into an animated once-a-day dialogue—albeit a written one.

"The *Daily News* pretty much filled you in on my personal history," I wrote. "Care to fill me in on yours?"

"Sure. I'm a divorced Jewish workaholic. I have three kids—all boys—who I'm very close to, great friends, and a cool job."

Professionally, Jack told me, he was the business manager for a music icon, but he felt more comfortable declaring himself an international drug smuggler because it caused less commotion.

"If I'm at a party I use the drug thing and stick with it until it makes people nervous. If I *really* don't want to speak to people I tell them I'm in insurance. I use that on airplanes a lot. God, this makes me sound so arrogant. But when people find out who I work for their eyes kind of glaze over and the questions start coming until I start to fake a coronary. I came up with most of this stuff when I moved to Westchester . . . all those white-water rafting, golf ball–whacking, arbitraging merger and acquisitioners seem to bring out the worst in me. Or maybe it's just that I like the spin."

I didn't blame Jack for his attempts at subterfuge. My fifteen minutes plus of fame had given me some insight into how he felt.

"That's funny," I replied. "I'm a publicist. My whole life is spin."

"But here's the million-dollar question," he wrote back. "Do you spin things to yourself in order to lessen the emotional impact? Or just to the outside world?"

I thought about my response for a while before pushing the Send button.

"I guess the answer is both. But I'm not so sure the spin lessens the emotional impact. I read a great quote the other day: 'One does not laugh because one is happy; one is happy because one laughs.' I find that philosophy—along with a new handbag every now and then—usually works pretty well for me. Best, Isabel."

"Excellent quote, although I'm afraid I've never really enjoyed a new handbag. Seeing my kids always cheers me up, though. The most important thing in life, right?"

There were many things I still didn't know about Jack. But at least, I thought, his response indicated that he valued his kids and was probably not a cross-dresser.

Although I had some experience with long-distance relationships, romances with friends, and even a flirtation with a second cousin, I had never had an e-mail relationship that was just . . . an e-mail relationship. There was a certain anonymity that was freeing; it didn't take a genius to realize that it was easier to be frank when you didn't really know the person you were being frank with. There were no expectations beyond a reply. There was no pressure, except possibly to be supportive, amusing, and a good speller.

When I didn't hear from Jack for a couple of days—we had been e-mailing daily for a couple of weeks by then—I assumed that he had met a flesh-and-blood girl and moved on. But that wasn't the case.

"I've been working 'round the clock," he wrote, "doing interviews, approving cover copy, and making myself crazy."

"Why do you work so hard?" I asked him.

"I dunno," he replied. "I guess I like the stress of long hours . . . what I call 'heavy work mode,' when things are buzzing, the phone is ringing, and you can't stop to think. It gives me the illusion that I'm accomplishing something."

"Sounds to me like a cover for loneliness."

"I'll level with you, Isabel. Sometimes it is. My marriage breaking up was very hard for me. But there comes a point when it's time to move on and make peace with what you have. I've reached that point. I never liked dating much. And I've learned that when you lose someone, your life usually expands in ways to accommodate the loss. Carpe diem is nice but it's tough to seize the day . . . no matter how hard you try it's always slipping through your fingers. But I have my work, my kids, my friends. And now I even have an e-mail pal. Who has time to be lonely?"

"Well . . . me, actually." Although I wasn't prepared to put the unabridged story into print, I was still trying to adjust to Tuesday nights without Charlie. That plus the upcoming holidays had done little to lift my mood. "I'm sick to death of hearing myself say it . . . let alone writing it," I confessed, "but I've been feeling kind of low these last few weeks."

"You should never downplay feeling bad," Jack responded. "I lost my dad when I was eighteen, my sister when I was twenty-one, and my wife when I was forty-three and came home early to find her stuffing clothes into a suitcase. If there's one thing I can tell you for sure, it's that life has its ups as well as its downs and everyone has the God-given right to feel sorry for themselves once in a while. Think of it as a necessary break from all the energy it takes to get through the day."

Unless he was bluffing—and at times I was almost certain he was—Jack seemed to have the suddenly single thing down pat, something I was still trying to get a handle on.

"You seem so well adjusted," I wrote him. "Got any suggestions?"

The next day he sent me the following:

TIPS ON GOING IT ALONE

1. FIND YOURSELF AMUSING
2. TALK TO YOURSELF WHILE YOU ARE DOING THINGS
3. ENJOY THE ASPECT OF DOING WHAT YOU WANT WHEN YOU WANT TO
4. BECOME A WORKAHOLIC WITH NO FREE TIME SO IT REALLY DOESN'T MAKE A DIFFERENCE

"You know, Izzy," said Wendy after reviewing the list, which I had forwarded to her via e-mail, "with the exception of tip number four, this kind of describes the homeless man I used to see every morning at 30th Street Station."

"Yeah, I considered that. But I asked Jack for the tips 'cause it's been a rough month. So, you know, when the going gets tough . . ."

". . . Izzy goes shopping."

"Right. So I'm at Marshalls this afternoon looking for shoes. As per tip number two, I'm talking to myself about the cute heels with the plastic fruit on them, and you know what? I really did feel better. Until . . ."

"Until?"

". . . until it hit me by the home furnishings aisle that both Jack and I will probably end up all alone, talking to ourselves with a house full of cats and a prize-winning string collection. Then the weirdest thing happened."

"What?"

"Well, Wendy . . . for the second time today . . . I actually laughed out loud."

In my next correspondence to Jack, I relayed my success with his tips, along with Wendy's skepticism.

"Like the homeless guy at 30th Street Station, huh?"

"Yup."

"And what do you think?" he asked.

"Well, who's to say the guy at 30th Street Station isn't happy in some small way? Anyway, it looks like the tips work for you. You seem," I wrote, "at least via e-mail, to be somewhat joyful. Or at least not depressed, which these days, without medication, is almost the same thing."

Jack's response shot back faster than his usual twelve or so hours.

"Never confuse being witty, funny, and/or amusing with being joyful, my friend. I love spending time with my kids. I love getting things done, meeting new people, and thinking about interesting things. But I'm not so sure about the joy."

Was he kidding? How could he come across so well adjusted on my computer screen but not be sure about the joy?

"But then what's the point?" I wrote him. "What's the point of being with your kids, getting things done, meeting new people, and thinking about interesting things?"

"Isabel, when I first wrote to you it was simply to acknowledge that I thought you did something happy and brave. I know from personal experience that it's not easy to put yourself out there after losing so much. But perhaps I'm just overworked . . ." (tip number four, I reflected) "and will be feeling the joy tomorrow. I actually have a very optimistic brand of pessimism. I don't think things will work out but I try so hard to make them happen. Ahh, the conflict. So, tell me a joyous moment for you. Can you remember a moment of sublime happiness?"

Sublime happiness? The blissful memories sprang forth fully formed. "My wedding day. My children being born. Yes, I can remember many moments of sublime happiness . . . but they are quite a distance away. However, Jack, I do think I'm pretty solid with the joy."

Wow, I thought to myself . . . when did that happen?

"I feel joy upon leaving the gym in the morning . . . knowing that I burned enough calories so that I can feel joy eating a buttered cinnamon raisin bagel. I felt joy the other day when I booked a client on Leno. I feel joy when I watch a *West Wing* rerun. I feel joy when I'm with my kids. I'm not talking nirvana here . . . just the little things that cause a smile."

And then I took a leap.

"I think you're bullshitting yourself, Jack. I don't know you well enough to be sure, but I think you *do* feel joy. But maybe, after all you've lost, it feels safer to bury it under a pile of work and not to acknowledge it. Because I don't think you could appreciate your kids or be so good at what you do if you didn't feel a passion for it. And you can't do passion, Jack, if you can't do joy."

I woke up the next morning to find no response from Jack. Perhaps, I thought, I unwittingly broke a rule in the E-mail Pal Handbook. Perhaps there *was* such a thing as getting too personal. As if in response to my thoughts and embarrassed by its tardiness, his e-mail slipped quietly into my in-box a few minutes later. I anxiously sat down in my leggings, T-shirt, and slippers to read it.

"I gave your last e-mail a lot of thought, Isabel. The thing is, I actually *do* enjoy my life. It might sometimes sound to the contrary because I'm not afraid of looking at the dark side (that's me—the Darth Vader of Tarrytown). As far as the 'joy' thing goes, maybe I just call what I feel something else. Perhaps there should be a new word for 'joy,' one that hasn't been used to describe a new diet soda or a dishwashing liquid. I am sure there is a German word for it. Germans have all these words for complex emotions, like *schadenfreude* (it means the delight in someone else's misfortune) . . . while Jews have the wonderful *naches,* one of the greatest emotions of all time."

Naches. I had heard the word before, but its definition escaped me. And then all at once I remembered.

"*Naches,*" the buff rabbi had told me at Michael's funeral. "One day again you'll feel joy."

Three New Years had come and gone since Michael died, and my life, I reflected, was finally getting back on track. That feeling lasted a full two weeks, until mid-January when the air got so cold it was downright hostile and Sadie began complaining of a stomachache that wouldn't go away. It didn't seem to be the result of the flu, a virus, or fast-food chili. There were no other symptoms, or if there were she wasn't telling. The first trip to the pediatrician yielded nothing but vague guessing. Then a week passed and she didn't improve. Going to the bathroom became torture. She would sit on the toilet and wrap her arms around my legs because she couldn't bear the pain.

The second time we went to the doctor, on a Friday, it was suggested that she might have a urinary tract infection. Tests were done, reassurances were made, and we went home to wait it out over the weekend.

"I Googled him," Phoebe informed me.

"You had nothing better to do?"

"If you want to know the truth, I'm considering an affair with the contractor."

"Really?"

"Possibly. If I like his work."

"I'm serious."

"I'm serious, too."

"With the contractor?"

"Why not? He's hardworking. Seems like a nice guy. Amazing biceps."

"I dunno. Just doesn't seem like a contractor would be your type."

"I'll tell you something, Iz. I've spent so much of my life trying to get to the top. Trying to find the perfect man, the perfect wardrobe, the perfect house in the perfect neighborhood. And now that I'm older and tired and not so cute anymore, I look around at where I ended up—divorced from the wrong guy, living in a rental back where I started from in New Jersey."

"And?"

"And . . . it's not so bad." I could imagine her shrugging her still flawless shoulders. "I've got a great job, great family, and great friends and—you know what?—the rest is not so important anymore. After rushing around my whole life I finally have time to sit around on a cold January weekend with a cup of coffee and some leftover cookies, read a back issue of *People* magazine, and Google my best friend's e-mail pal if I want to."

"OK, I'll bite. What'd you find out?"

I could hear Phoebe digging in on the other end of the line as she warmed to her subject.

"He's very impressive. I wouldn't be surprised if he drove a Porsche."

"Whatever."

"What do you mean 'whatever'? Maybe he's *The Guy*."

"What guy?"

"Don't be an ass, Izzy. "You know . . . magic number twenty-eight? *The Guy.*"

"That would be all well and good, Phoeb, but I think Jack's only number twenty-five."

"Twenty-five, huh? Wasn't that how old you were when you moved to New York?"

"Yeah. I was. Come to think of it, that psychic said something about number twenty-five."

"But your mom said it would be number twenty-eight."

"Oh that's good, Phoeb. My future will be determined either by my mother's morning talk-show survey or by a woman who talks to dead people."

"Stranger things have happened, my friend. But all things considered, I'm putting my money on the psychic."

"You leave your money right where it is!"

"Why are you getting so upset?"

Pause.

"It's him, isn't it? Jack really is The Guy!"

"Will ya stop it with The Guy! You told me two months ago I didn't need The Guy! You told me to sit on a bench and take a breath!"

"What are you doing over there? Taking notes? I told you to stop looking. I didn't say anything about what to do if he falls into your lap!"

"Right now I'm just worried about Sadie's stomachache. And besides, when Jack talks about how involved he is in his work, he sounds just like Michael. And Charlie."

"Charlie if he had a job. And a *way* better car."

"Whatever. So . . . was there a picture?"

"No. And I thought you're weren't interested."

"I'm not. Look, you know that after Michael died I was terrified of being alone. I thought that if I tried hard enough I could find a nice man, introduce him to the kids, take him to Passover, and move him into the apartment like a new set of bath towels. Now I realize it's not gonna be so easy."

"Why? Jack doesn't like matzos?"

"Funny, Phoebe."

"I'm serious, Izzy. You say you're not interested and I just thought . . . maybe that's why you keep dating the same guy."

"What do you mean?"

"I mean first there was Charlie, who aside from being virtually invisible was emotionally unavailable. And now you have this cyber thing going on . . ."

"It's not a cyber thing. Jack and I are friends."

"You don't need more friends, Izzy. You need The Guy."

But I was no longer sure. Manless in Montclair I might be, but I was feeling better about myself and my life than I had since before Michael died.

Since before as far back as I could remember.

Besides, I reasoned, both Jack and I were comfortable with our relationship's practical simplicity, as well as its possible limitations. And neither one of us seemed to be in much of a rush to alter it. Although Jack knew what I looked like from my *Daily News* mug shot, I hadn't even asked for his photo.

But life, being all about change, brings its own pressures, and after all those e-mails we scheduled an inevitable first phone call for the following week.

"You know I'm not in much of a rush to hear your voice," I wrote him. "Your laugh . . . definitely . . . but not so much your voice."

"Really? Why not?"

"Did you ever see *Gone with the Wind*?"

"Of course," he responded. "Why?"

"I liked the book better."

The results of Sadie's tests came back that Monday—negative—and it was suggested I consult a urologist. The pediatrician recommended a doctor, and an appointment was scheduled for noon on Tuesday, the following day.

I dropped Jenna at school and arranged for Ivana to pick her up should we run late. The doctor's office was a twenty-minute drive from the apartment. Sadie, despite her pain, spent the time looking out the window and talking to the clouds. When we arrived at the urologist's office, the waiting room was full but, as was her habit, Sadie took it in stride. On the way out the door that morning, I had grabbed a handful of toy catalogs from my mailbox, and Sadie skimmed through them while we sat. I filled out a monstrous amount of paperwork; half an hour later they took us in for the first procedure, a sonogram. The test went smoothly. After it was over, we returned to the waiting room. Half an hour after that, word came that they wanted to do another test.

I was handed a large cup of hot pink muck for Sadie to drink. She took a small sip and wrinkled her nose.

"It's yucky!"

"I know."

Her lips were pink. At that point we had been at the doctor's office for two hours.

"Why do they call it a cat scan? Are there kitties in there?"

"No kitties. Just a machine."

"A machine?"

"It won't hurt, honey. I promise. They're just going to check to see why your tummy hurts. Now please drink the yucky stuff."

"I don't wanna."

"I know, honey. But you have to. Look. I'll make a deal with you. You drink all that yucky stuff and I promise to buy you anything you want in any of the catalogs."

"Anything?"

"Anything."

It took her twenty minutes to drink three-quarters of the goo, and by that time she looked as if she might throw up. Before she had the chance we were led into a clinical-looking room with a giant CAT scan standing in the center, eating up most of the space.

The technicians spoke to Sadie kindly as they strapped her to the table and then slid her in for the scan. She was scared and she was tired and she held my hand tight, but Sadie was nothing if not brave.

She looked warily up at the machine that would take pictures of the inside of her tiny tummy.

"Anything I want, right?"

"Anything."

At 6:30 that evening, six and a half hours after we arrived, the urologist—a tall man with an easy manner—finally called us into his office. He smiled when we walked in.

I didn't consider it a good sign.

I sat down in the chair in front of his desk, and Sadie wandered off to explore. Dr. Mason leaned back in his leather chair and took a breath.

Another bad sign.

I looked around the office. It was decorated in the usual manner—family photos, notes and drawings from presumably happy patients, and some mostly broken toys in the corner that Sadie was now busy playing with.

"So," the doctor said, getting my attention. "How's your support system?"

"My what?"

"Your support system. You know . . . family, friends."

"Well, I'll tell you, doctor. My husband died a couple of years ago, my parents are lovely people but can't stand to be in the same state together, my best friend's divorce was recently finalized, and I'm still not over the guy who was helping me out of the hole but refused to commit. Why do you ask?"

"Well," Dr. Mason said, clearly unsure if he should continue. "I'll tell you." He glanced at Sadie. "We have a problem here."

"What kind of problem?" At this point I was in no mood for a good news/bad news conversation. I was tired. I was worried. And I wanted it straight.

"Your daughter has a tumor in her left ovary."

"A tumor? In her left ovary?" I blinked.

So much for the bad news. Sadie, my little bubble child, the kid with the huge brown eyes and no fear. The one who floated along to some tune in her head that only she could hear and often sang along with. Sadie had a tumor in her ovary.

She was six.

"My mom said she's going to get me the barrel of doggies," she told the doctor, catalog in hand. "There must be, like, a *thousand* doggies in there!"

He smiled at her and then looked back at me, the smile fading fast.

"She needs surgery. Immediately. Either I can do it or you could look for someone else. But it should be done soon."

I nodded my head. I thanked him. I took Sadie's hand and gathered my things and got into my car to drive home. Sadie quickly fell asleep in her car seat and, amid her snores, I called my mother with the news. Then I hung up the phone, pulled over to the right shoulder, and left the entire contents of my stomach by the side of the road.

It had been a tough couple of years by any measure, but I wasn't complaining. You did what you had to do and you kept on moving. My father had taught me that lesson and Michael had, too. But if this was another test—or possibly just someone's idea of a good time—I simply wasn't having any. So, in a strong clear voice, as cars whizzed by me on that cold, dark night, I told Michael and God right up front. I would raise two kids and support them on my own. I would, if I had to, spend the rest of my life as a single mother. I would even lay off shoe and handbag shopping. *But,* if they took Sadie, all bets were off. In fact, I told them, if they took Sadie, I was coming along, too.

CHAPTER SIXTEEN

Jordan and David were at my side before the next day was out. Ivana suggested a doctor at a nearby hospital. His reputation was excellent, but he was cold as a glacier and at this point I felt that Sadie and I were in need of a little handholding. He took a look at Sadie's CAT scan and offered the opinion that the tumor was in her bladder. I felt what little balance I had accrued over the past couple of years quickly slipping away. I wasn't a doctor, but I knew the basic facts. A person could live with one ovary. But without a bladder Sadie would be screwed.

Jordan knew of a surgeon in the city. After hearing the urgency of my situation, the nurse was kind enough to fit me in the following day. Sadie, who had once been the "plump" child, was now practically skin and bones. She was hardly eating or drinking, having figured out that what went in would eventually come out, painfully, on the other side.

Wendy drove up from Doylestown on Thursday morning to go with Sadie and me to meet the doctor while Jenna waited patiently at home with Ivana.

"Will Sadie die, too?" Jenna whispered to me as we headed for the door.

"Of course not," I lied through gritted teeth. God couldn't be so cruel.

We arrived at the hospital and were ushered into a cross between an office and a children's playroom to wait while the new doctor took a look at the CAT scan. He came in a few minutes later, a handsome man in his late forties, exuding warmth and reassurance. He had a short conversation with Sadie first, and I knew right then that this was the guy for us.

While Sadie busied herself with the toys, Dr. Stevens told Wendy and me that the tumor may indeed involve her bladder. But then again, he said, it may not. CAT scans were tricky, and it wasn't a good idea to predict the outcome from them. He said that he could schedule Sadie's surgery for the following morning except for one thing. Sadie had developed the sniffles and a slightly runny nose. If she had a problem breathing in the morning, they wouldn't be able to operate.

We arrived at the hospital the next morning while it was still dark. Sadie was a little nervous but happy at the prospect of finally getting rid of the pain. It had been a little over a month since her stomach had started to ache.

David was there when we arrived. He went with me into the small changing room where they would check us in and get Sadie's vitals.

"She's still got the runny nose," I said, pacing. "What if they won't take her?"

He was sitting on the chair with his arms wrapped protectively around his sister. David, who had always possessed the makings of a family man, yearned for one of his own. During the time he spent with my kids, it was easy to see that he would make a great dad. But, like me, he needed to find a partner first.

"The pain in her belly is worse than the runny nose. Don't you worry," David said confidently. "They'll take her."

"You're a great guy, David," I told him, not for the first time.

"And a great big brother!" chimed in Sadie, leaning into his chest.

"That's what family is for," David said, giving Sadie a gentle squeeze.

The nurse came in a few minutes later.

"Hello, Mr. and Mrs. Ackerman. This must be Sadie."

Although I always thought David bore a stronger resemblance to his mother, there was certainly more than a little bit of Michael in him. The same blue eyes and sandy hair. The same "I'll protect my family at all costs" vibe. But David was taller and wirier than Michael and a good twenty-five years younger.

Before I could respond to the nurse, Sadie jumped in. "Oh, no," she said with a laugh. "That's not my dad! My dad's in heaven now. This is my brother. David."

The nurse smiled, lifted Sadie onto the examining table, and stuck a thermometer into her mouth. She had a temperature of 99.1.

"She usually runs a little above normal," David told the nurse confidently. "And the runny nose is mostly from allergies." I shot him a look. How the heck did he know?

"OK," the nurse responded. "In any case it's not enough to delay the surgery." David looked at me and smiled. I breathed. Sadie jumped off the table.

We were on.

By the time they took her into surgery, the waiting room was flooded with family and friends. My parents, shockingly, seemed to be conducting a civil conversation, their heads bent toward each other in grandparently concern. Wendy, having left Arnie in charge of the kids, stared blankly at the TV overhead. Jordan, in an effort to keep informed, was chatting up the nurses, and Phoebe, having taken a day off from work, was curled up in the corner with her BlackBerry. I wasn't sure if they had bribed the guards or crept in when no one was looking, but my support group certainly exceeded the number of people allowed.

Three hours later the surgeon appeared and asked me to follow him into a smaller room. My knees buckled slightly as I stood. Wendy grabbed me by the elbow and helped me walk, as I'd done with her when she was two.

"Sadie had a massive infection that I believe we completely removed. We're calling it a pseudo-tumor. Essentially, her body created it to protect itself from spreading the infection."

Wendy took a deep breath. "What about her ovaries?" she asked.

"Perfectly intact. Both of them."

"And her bladder?" I asked, voice shaking.

"Fine. Everything's fine. We'll have the pathology report in a week or so. At that point we'll know for sure about the tumor."

"What else?" I asked. Because I was sure there was another shoe somewhere just waiting to be dropped.

"Well, we took a quick look through her navel before making the incision. Good thing too, because based on the scan it looked like I needed to do a horizontal cut. But after we took a look we realized it was better to do a vertical one. It's about two inches in length."

"And that's it?"

He smiled at me. "Oh, I'm sure that's enough. She's going to be mighty angry when she wakes up and in quite a bit of pain."

"Angry?" I asked curiously.

"Angry."

After what seemed like many hours I was finally allowed into the recovery room to see my baby. She was as pale as the sheets she was lying on, her bowl-cut, dark brown hair fanned out behind her. She had an IV tube in her arm, and there were spots of blood on the bedding. I went over and stroked her head. Her eyes opened slowly at my touch. Her lips were dry, and she talked in a whisper. I leaned down close to hear her.

"I'm mad," she said. "Really, really mad!"

Then she closed her eyes and fell back to sleep.

And it was then I heard God say, in a voice very much like my father's, "Buck up, Isabel Louise. You may not have a husband but at least Sadie's going to be OK. And things could always, *always,* be worse."

When Sadie next woke up, she was more lucid and much *much* angrier. "It hurts! It hurts!" she cried. I begged the nurses for more painkillers, but it seemed like forever until they came. Shortly thereafter we were moved to a semiprivate room where Sadie, connected to a web of tubes and monitors, latched onto my hair and refused to let go.

By nine that evening my parents and Wendy had gone to fetch Jenna from Ivana's, where she would stay for the next few days, to her delight, for a record-breaking long playdate with Austin. Jordan, David, and Phoebe, too wired to call it a day, decided they needed some sustenance besides the chips and Tastycake available in the omnipresent vending machines. To celebrate the success of the surgery, they decided to dine at a steak restaurant downtown—known for the heifer on its roof and the size of its portions. On their way out I asked them to bring me a doggy bag; they returned with a roast beef the size of a small child. As there were no plates big enough on which to place it, I ended up taking small bites out of a sterilized bedpan.

Sadie and I remained at the hospital for the next four days. There was only one bed in her room. Beside it was a chair that, in theory, folded out into something resembling a bed. In reality a contortionist would have had a problem finding a comfy spot. In any case, Sadie was loath to let go of my hair, so sleep for both of us remained at a minimum.

After the first night she was hooked up to a morphine drip to control the pain. Thanks to my family and friends, I got some of New York's finest cuisine delivered bedside.

I *really* would have preferred the morphine.

Charlie checked in periodically by cell phone. He asked me to send Sadie his best wishes. He assured me that he'd love to come and visit, but said he knew I was surrounded by family and friends so his presence wasn't really required. He was right, of course. But he was also consistent. He had an excuse, and he latched onto it as a reason not to be present in my life when I needed him. He couldn't, or wouldn't, move out of his own world, even if it were just to share in mine.

In the past when this type of thing happened with Charlie, I'd feel hurt and rejected. Maybe it was my fault he didn't love me enough. Maybe *I* should try harder. But this time it was different. Just living, I thought, could be sufficiently painful. I didn't need to chase any extra heartache from Charlie.

Sadie's stay in the hospital not only cured her but also cured me. God had taken me by the shoulders and shaken me—hard. I finally found the strength to stand up without falling over, and I realized that I needed nothing more than what I had. In fact, when I thought about it—and in those four days I had plenty of time to do so—I had more, even without Michael, than I had ever dreamed.

Sublime happiness, Jack had written, *fleeting moments of perfection you get once or twice in a lifetime.*

On day four at noon, Sadie got her discharge papers. I lifted her gently out of bed, hugged her skinny body in my arms for a moment, and then settled her into a wheelchair. She refused to take the morphine orally; after they discontinued the drip, she decided that the pain was more bearable than the taste of the medicine.

We rolled down the hall, gratefully bidding adieu to the nice nurses, antiseptic smells, and shiny floors. I followed the signs and headed toward the elevators, going at a respectable speed despite Sadie's wish to race. Nevertheless—and true to my miserable driving record—I crashed into someone as I rounded the corner. Sadie winced.

It had been four days since I'd had a proper shower and over a week since I'd had a decent night's sleep. I was happy and grateful to be taking my baby home, but I was in no mood for idiots who couldn't avoid a six-year-old in a wheelchair.

"Jeez, man! Watch where you're going! This is a hospital, not a speedway!" I leaned over the back of the chair to make sure Sadie was okay.

"That was fun!" she said. "Do it again!"

I couldn't help but smile at her unflagging enthusiasm. The culprit—about 5'9" with curly dark brown hair—knelt down in front of Sadie.

"So you want to do it again?" he asked her sweetly. "Do you really think that's such a good idea? I mean considering your tummy and all?"

Sadie giggled.

His eyes, when he looked up at me, were a shade of blue I hadn't seen since Michael's.

"Maybe, if your mom says it's OK, we can meet back here in a few weeks. I'll get my own wheelchair and we can have a proper race. What do you say to that?"

Sadie looked back up to me. "Can we, Mama? Can we?"

It would sound too much like a children's fairy tale for me to say that when I looked into his eyes that first time I knew he was the man I was no longer looking for. It would sound like a fairy tale.

But it certainly would be true.

He stood up and extended his hand.

"I'm Jack. Isabel and Sadie, I presume?"

My first real-time conversation with Jack was supposed to happen the week before. But with Sadie so ill, who had the time to think about a phone call?

"When you stopped e-mailing, I figured something must be up. I'm not sure what it says in the E-mail Pal Guidebook," he said with a shy smile, "but I didn't think you knew me well enough just to dump me."

"But how did you know I'd be here?"

"I called your place this morning and spoke to your mom. She said she was there making sure everything was ready for Sadie's homecoming. I asked 'homecoming from where?' When she told me what was going on, I figured maybe I'd grab a cab and come on over."

"What about 'heavy work mode'?"

"Let's just say I rearranged things. An e-mail friend of mine helped me realize that there are some things more important than a work schedule."

Sadie's final pathology report came back a week later on what would have been Michael's fifty-eighth birthday. We had already planned to commemorate the occasion. Now we could send the good news—Sadie's tumor contained no traces of cancer—up with the balloons. Sadie, Jenna, and I set out at noon. The day was bright and cold, and we were bundled up to the point of immobility. The breeze in the backyard pulled at the brightly colored orbs as we tried to maneuver them away from the bare tree branches.

"Now? Can we let go now?" asked Sadie, her breath visible in the cold winter air. It was her first outing since arriving home, and her recovery had been no less than miraculous.

"Yes," I told my girls. "You can let go now."

As the string slipped through my fingers and I watched our balloons ascend to the sky, I had a sudden realization of how much I had changed. Maybe not in terms as measurable as *better* or *worse*, but I was certainly not the same Isabel I had been before that hot August day when I left my husband at home with a headache to go get my teeth whitened.

It had been a long road. But I had finally realized that the secret of surviving was to embrace the change instead of running from it, to trust that magic was still possible even though it was sometimes buried under considerable amounts of pain and debris.

Good thing I had learned how to handle a shovel.

EPILOGUE

It was the first night of Passover, and I sat perched on the steps leading from the living room to the second floor of Wendy and Arnie's house, talking with Jordan about life.

"I may not be gorgeous, Izzy, but I am a *little* attractive, don't you think?"

"Stop fishing, Jordy. You know you're gorgeous."

"Oh, go *on*.

Pause.

"No, really," he said, as I knew he would, "go on!"

"Arnie's starting the service in ten minutes, Jordan, so why don't we skip the superficial flattery and get right to the problem?"

"Same problem. When will I find a nice guy and settle down? All my friends are in relationships. All my parents are remarried . . . except for you. Why can't I find someone?"

It was a good question. Jordan was undoubtedly one of the best people I knew. He helped with the kids, offered smart advice for almost any dilemma I found myself in, and knew the words to nearly every Shania Twain song ever recorded. And he wasn't looking for perfection. Just a nice man who shared his wish for a nicely decorated home, a stylish wardrobe, and a couple of kids.

"What's the matter with me?" he groaned.

"I'll tell you a little secret, honey. It's not like . . . say . . . cooking. You can't rush it."

"Since when do you cook?"

"I don't. Bad analogy. OK, let's try this one. Last week in the shower I had an epiphany."

"I think this conversation just fell under the heading of 'way too much information.' "

"An epiphany, Jordan. A realization."

"Right," he said, reaching in his pocket for a piece of gum. "I knew that."

"There I was . . . washing my hair and thinking about Tarzan."

"Tarzan?"

"Yeah. You know . . . the jungle guy who swings through the trees?"

"I know who Tarzan is, Isabel. And I think that Clairol may be putting one too many herbs into your shampoo."

"Seriously, Jordy. I was thinking about when he swung through the trees . . . how he had to let go of the vine he was holding on to in order to reach the vines that were out in front. How he had to trust that he wouldn't fall and that there would be another vine to carry him even if he couldn't see it right away."

"Is there a message here, Izzy? Because if I'm not mistaken there are only seven nights of Passover."

"Yeah. There's a message. You'll meet a guy when you're ready and you'll settle down when it's time. The message is that things change. I wouldn't have the same relationship I have now with Jenna and Sadie if Michael hadn't died. I wouldn't have the same appreciation of my family and friends. I wouldn't have met Charlie."

"Forget about Charlie."

"But that's my point, Jordan. Michael *led* me to Charlie. And Charlie helped lead me to Isabel . . . Isabel on her own. And that's what led me to Jack."

I glanced over to where my boyfriend sat talking to Wendy on the couch while Sadie, now fully recovered, tried to balance a matzo ball on her head. Jack and I had been dating since a week after we officially met at the hospital. There had been adjustments, of course. But overall he had slipped into our lives as easily as Michael had slipped into mine all those years ago.

"So anyway," I went on, "I jumped out of the shower, ran into the bedroom, and grabbed a lipstick from my dresser. I stood in front of the mirror and wrote a reminder for myself . . . *Trust the Universe.*"

"You're making this up."

"Ask Jenna. She came in a couple of minutes later, read the message, told me I was crazy, and asked me how long I planned to keep it there."

"What'd you say?"

"As long as I needed reminding. Because I'll tell you something . . . this journey thing? It's not just about how much power

AMY HOLMAN EDELMAN

you have or what kind of car you drive. It's about best friends. And
family. And e-mail pals. It's about the people you meet, the people
you love, and the people who love you back. It's about stupid
clichés like 'You're never alone if you have friends,' 'The glass is
half full,' and 'Life is a cabaret.' "

"Are you gonna sing a show tune, Izzy? Because I don't think
I can handle it if you're gonna sing a show tune."

"No show tunes, Jordy. Just this—in the end . . . it's all about
naches."

"God bless you."

"I didn't sneeze, Jordan. It's about how much joy you get out
of the trip."

ABOUT THE AUTHOR

Amy Holman Edelman lives in New Jersey with her husband, children, and Irish Jack Russell, Roxy.

ABOUT THE TYPE

This book was set in Dante MT, redrawn in 1957 by Ron Carpenter for the Monotype Corporation. Giovanni Mardersteig designed the original Dante after World War II at the Officina Bodoni. Mardersteig's Dante was created in collaboration with Charles Malin, a renowned punch-cutter. Their goal was a lively, legible, and attractive book face. The subtle stress that is created by the serifs and top curves of the characters enhance legibility. Dante is the culmination of this collaborative period, and is recognized as Mardersteig's most successful design.